RAIRARUBIA

**UNCORRECTED
PRE-PUBLICATION COPY;
NOT FOR DISTRIBUTION
OR SALE.**

W. Royce Adams

LOST≈≈≈
COAST
PRESS
Fort Bragg
California

RAIRARUBIA

Library of Congress Cataloging-in-Publication Data

Adams, W. Royce.
  Rairarubia / W. Royce Adams. — 1st ed.
        p. cm.
  Summary: When her father starts making up stories about a girl named Romey in the magical land of Rairarubia, eleven-year-old Molly finds herself crossing over into that land and sharing in Romey's adventures.
  ISBN: 1-882897-36-6
  [1. Storytelling Fiction. 2. Fantasy.] I. Title
PZ7.A2188Rai 1999
[Fic]—dc21   99-21436
                                                   CIP

For more information, or to order additional copies, please contact the publisher:
Lost Coast Press
155 Cypress Street
Fort Bragg CA 95437
1-800-773-7782

Book production by Cypress House
Printed in Canada

First edition

10 9 8 7 6 5 4 3 2 1

For my daughter, Kate Brody-Adams, who asked me to write something fun to read.

RAIRARUBIA

CHAPTER 1

Molly Doogan sat on her bedroom floor next to her opened dresser drawer unaware of the warm tears sliding down her flushed cheeks.

"No! Please! Not again!" she wanted to shout, but couldn't. If her parents heard her, they'd come to her room, and then they'd want to know what was wrong. Then she'd have to tell them about what she'd found before and kept hidden in her drawer—about the things that were happening to her that she couldn't explain.

And now these. She looked at the pebbles in one hand and the small leather pouch in the other.

It was all too confusing. Things like this aren't supposed to happen in real life. But what was real and what wasn't? She wasn't sure any more. She felt like she was living in two different dimensions.

And all because of that night—that night she and her dad sat in the car waiting for her mother...

"Your mom's *really* late tonight."

Molly noticed her father eye the Volvo's dashboard clock for only about the two hundredth time. She could tell he was bored, too. But nowhere near as bored as she was. Forever—that's how long it felt they'd been waiting in the medical clinic's parking lot. Forever and a day.

Molly let out a noisy sigh to let her father know her impatience. Now that she'd turned eleven, she tried to be less fidgety, act more mature. But she thought she would explode into a kazillion pieces or something if her mother didn't walk out the clinic door soon.

"Guess your mom had a lot of patients today, what with the flu going around." She saw her dad look at the clock again. That made two hundred and one.

Except for times like this, Molly liked having a doctor mother. She always got a little kick when she heard, "Calling Dr. Doogan. Calling Dr. Doogan," on the clinic speakers. Sometimes at home when her mother called her, she'd answer with, "What's up, doc?" But right now she wished her mother was a bank clerk, or a librarian, or a teacher even—some job with a more regular schedule.

Molly tried squirming into a more comfortable position. Nothing worked. Then she searched through the glove compartment but found nothing but a burnt out flashlight, some broken pencils, a tattered map, and a hair clip she thought she'd lost.

Using the clip, she pulled her light-brown hair into a ponytail. Then she twisted the rearview mirror and switched on the overhead light so she could see herself. She turned her head from side to side, then stuck her tongue out at herself.

"You know, you have your mother's blue eyes. And with your hair pulled back like that, you're looking more and more like her."

Realizing her dad had been watching her, Molly blushed. "Well, I wish mom would come out that door right this minute. She's never been this late before."

Molly began fiddling with the radio, punching buttons and changing stations every few seconds. Almost every station had either news, classical music, freeway alerts, or loud commercials. As soon as a station played music she didn't like, she switched to another.

"Molly, must you?"

"But I'm bored, daddy."

"I know, I know."

Molly watched him take off his glasses, hold them up, sigh, rub his nose, and put his glasses on. "But if you can't find something you like, turn it off, okay, kiddo?"

When her dad called her "kiddo," she knew he wasn't really angry.

"I will—if you tell me a story."

Molly hoped he'd say yes, but he just smiled at her for a moment, his brown eyes peering over his black-rimmed glasses.

"A story, huh?"

"Please? It'll help pass the time for you, too."

"What kind of story?"

"I don't know. Make one up." Molly placed her hands together prayer-like and made a silly, pleading face. "Please, please, please."

"Hey, now, kiddo, easier said than done." Her father smiled and looked through the windshield at the clinic doorway. Molly sensed he was hoping her mother would show up now so he could get out of telling a story.

"Why should it be so hard? You're a writer. You're always writing those manuals and stuff for your work."

"Well, that's a little different. That's technical 'stuff,' as you call it, not stories."

"Oh, come on, dad," she coaxed, tucking on his arm, "just a little one 'til mom comes." She pulled her knees up to her chin, pressed her back against the car door so she could face him, and widened her blue eyes in expectation.

"Oookay," he stretched out the word, "but only if you help me."

"Help? How?"

"Well, like, when should the story take place? In the present, the past, the future?"

Molly thought a moment. "Maybe the past—sort of."

Her father nodded. "The past—sort of. All right. Now then, where?"

"You mean, where in the world?"

3

"The world, or anywhere you like. It could be here on earth but maybe an unknown world, out in space, some place unusual —rare. Make it up."

Molly fell quiet for a moment. Then, "How about Raresville? That sounds rare and different." She laughed at herself.

"Raresville, hmm? Not bad. Do you know what 'ville' means?"

"I think so. Small town or village, right?"

"Right. So, do you want the story to take place in a small village or some place bigger?" She saw him look out toward the clinic door.

"Bigger, for sure. And let's make it a really pretty place—lots of mountains and hills and valleys—clean rivers, lakes, and air—lots of jewels—rubies mostly."

"Okay. Give it a name."

Molly ran her fingers through her ponytail, then said excitedly, "I know! How about a place called Rairarubia?"

"Rairarubia," her father repeated. "Hmm. I like that. Rairarubia."

"Rare, air, rubies. Get it?"

"Oh, I get it," her dad laughed. "Very clever. Okay, Rairarubia it is. Hey, maybe you should be telling me a story." Her father gave a gentle tug on Molly's ponytail.

"No, no. Together. But you mostly." Molly twisted around to get more comfortable.

"Well, let's see now. We're in Rairarubia sometime in the past, sort of. Where do we start? In the mountains, on the river, the hills? Where?"

Molly's brow knitted in thought. "Hm. What do you think?"

Her father gazed out the windshield again, but she could tell he was thinking, not looking, this time. "How about this. It can change as we move along in the story. We'll let our imaginations take over. So, let's start with a lush, green valley spotted with huge oak, elm, and sycamore trees. A blue-green lake forms at one end, so clear you can see right to the deep bottom. At the other end of the valley, rolling green hills give way to high, snow-topped mountains. A fast running river runs down from the mountains and spills into the lake. Sound good?"

"Yeah, that sounds pretty. I like it."

"But we don't have any people."

"Oh, yeah. We've got to have people."

"So who's in the story? Make up someone."

"OK. Let's see. Well, there's a girl, of course."

"Of course."

"Her name is—Romey."

"Romey. Good name. What's she look like?"

"Well, she's got short, dark hair and blue-green eyes. She's twelve, no, thirteen—and tall for her age."

"Okay, now, how is she dressed?"

"Hmm. Let's see." Molly ran her fingers through her hair again. "How about a yellow T-shirt and overall jeans, with straps, the kind I told you and mom I want to get. And she's wearing AirWalks, like me." Molly paused, then added, "Romey's also very strong. She could even beat you in arm wrestling." Molly gently elbowed her dad.

"Ah, well, I'll be sure to stay on the good side of this girl," her father laughed. "Any one else around?"

Molly thought for a moment, checking to see if the woman coming out of the door was her mother, but it wasn't. "No, she's walking alone along the river."

"Why? Is she lost? Sad?"

Molly thought a minute. "No. She doesn't know why she's there. She has no memory. She's wondering what we're going to do with her." Molly smiled, wondering herself.

"Ah, I see. Well, let's not keep her waiting."

"You begin it." Molly settled back in the seat, no longer bored.

"Hmm. Well, there she is walking along the river, wondering how she got there when..."

Romey, walking along the river, suddenly saw a huge shadow cast from overhead racing along the ground toward her. She looked up and gasped. A gigantic, maroon-colored bird, very much like a pterodactyl, only thick with rainbow colored feathers, dropped into a silent glide. Before she could blink, it swooped her off in its claws and headed for the mountains.

At first, Romey screamed and tried to wiggle free, but the higher they flew, the more she realized she'd better not move or she'd fall. The bird's huge, stretched-out wings swished with such a terrible racket as it flapped upward that she had to hold her hands over her ears.

She could see little because of the forceful wind in her face, but as she squinted downward, she noticed everything below growing smaller and smaller. The river looked like a thin blue ribbon dropped to the floor, the lake just an ink splot. Then all she could see was the broken shadow of the bird as it flew above the snow-covered mountains behind the lake.

The bird began to bank and zigzag between mountain peaks. The longer they flew, the colder Romey got. Only the bird's huge scratchy claws wrapped around her kept her from freezing.

Then, without warning, the bird's claws opened!

Romey screamed as she fell through the cold air thinking surely her life was over.

But, of course, it wasn't.

She landed in something soft and bounced twice before settling still. Under other conditions it might have been fun, like bouncing on a trampoline. But Romey found nothing funny about any of this. Especially when she noticed she was sitting between two huge, dirty-white objects splattered with purple specks. Upon a closer look, Romey realized what they were.

Eggs, twice her size!

"The bird's nest!" Romey said to herself. "I'm in the

bird's nest."

Then it dawned on her. "And I'm supposed to be the first meal for its chicks!"

Romey looked around for a way out, but the dark shadow of the bird overhead dimmed the light. Then she found herself slipping into near total darkness as the bird gently sat on her and the eggs.

Once again she thought she was doomed, but fortunately the bird's nest was so big and soft that Romey found she had room to crawl through the moss-like nest. Careful not to disturb the bird, she worked her way out from under the feathered giant by pulling herself upward toward a speck of light at the rim of the huge nest. Luckily, Romey came out at the bird's back so it didn't see her.

Once out, though, she had no idea what to do next. It was cold without the warmth of the bird. She folded her arms across her chest and shivered.

"How am I going to get out of this mess?" she muttered to herself.

As she looked for some way to escape, Romey noticed some loose feathers lying about. Being a huge bird, some feathers were rather large. Very slowly, so the bird wouldn't feel her movements, she pulled several toward her thinking she might be able to use them to cover herself for warmth.

While gathering feathers, she noticed something gleaming embedded deeper in the nest. She pulled and untwisted the object from the nest fibers and discovered a gold necklace. The chain, made of strong, solid links, had a large, oval-shaped medallion attached. As Romey examined the medallion, she noticed four deep indentations, each one a different shape. It appeared jewels had been taken from it. The bird, Romey guessed, must have gathered up the necklace as part of its nest building.

Romey's first concern was to get warm, so with a shrug of her shoulders, she slipped the necklace over her head and turned back to gathering feathers.

She fashioned the feathers into a bulky, cape-like covering. Then she tied it together with thin fibers the bird had also collected in making up the nest. Awkward or not, the feathered cape felt warm against her skin.

"Much better. Now, how do I get out of here?" she asked herself.

Romey eased herself up the side of the nest toward the rim. She scooted backwards so she could keep an eye on the bird's back without disturbing it. With her clumsy cape, it seemed a lifetime before she made her way up.

Reaching the rim she looked down. She bit her lip to keep from yelling out. Her side of the nest, set into a small ledge on the mountain, hung out over a thirty foot drop into the snow below. There seemed no way to get out of the nest on this side. She didn't dare try to crawl around to the other side for fear the bird would see her or feel her move.

After a moment's thought, Romey started pulling loose some of the rope-like fibers that made up the bottom of the nest. Still taking care not to disturb the bird, she began tying together as many pieces of fiber as she could until she had fashioned a long rope. Once finished, she tied one end to the biggest and sturdiest part of the bird nest she could find. Slowly, she let out her rope over the edge of the nest.

"Well, here goes everything," Romey whispered to herself. "Bird, please take a little nap."

Romey crept over the side of the nest and began letting herself down the fiber rope hand-over-hand. Being strong, this was no problem for Romey. The problem was that her fashioned rope wasn't long enough. When she looked down, everything was too white and bright from the snow. She had no idea how much farther she had to go.

For a moment, Romey just hung there, feet dangling. "Well," she told herself, "it's back up or let go."

She let go.

After a short drop, she felt her feet sinking into deep snow.

But just as she was feeling free of the bird, she heard it give an ear-piercing squawk. Then she could see the shadow of its huge wings on the snow. She looked up and saw the bird rise from its nest and circle her. Her feet didn't have to be told to move.

Knee deep in snow, Romey trudged as fast as she could toward a small cut in the mountain that she thought might hide her. But her bulky feather cape and thick snow made it difficult to move.

The shadow of the bird drew nearer and wider.

"I've got to make it, I've got to," she muttered half aloud, drawing deep, hard breaths.

But she didn't.

Just as the bird swooped in, the snow under Romey gave way. She found herself falling, then sliding down . . . down . . . down . . . faster and faster, her breath leaving her. She felt like a balloon with its air escaping, twirling, swirling, down and around, down, down through a tunnel of white . . .

"Hey, you two, sorry to be so late."

Molly and her father had been so wrapped up in the story they hadn't noticed Molly's mother had left the clinic. She smiled at them through the car window.

"Oh, please don't stop the story now, daddy," Molly pleaded as she climbed into the back seat making room for her mother.

"What story?" her mother said as she got into the car. "And what about a 'Hello, mommy, glad-to-see-you-did-you-have-a-good-day'?"

"Hi, mom. Sorry. 'Course I'm glad to see you. It's just that dad and I are in the middle of a story, and it's just getting good." Molly couldn't conceal her disappointment, even though she really was happy to see her mother.

"We can continue the story later. You start thinking of what might come next." Her father leaned over and greeted his wife with a kiss on the cheek as he started the car.

"But when? Bet we never finish it now," Molly muttered as she fastened her seat belt.

"Oh, I don't know," her dad said. "I'm getting rather fond of Romey myself."

"And just who is Romey?" his wife asked. "Should I be jealous?"

Molly looked in the rear view mirror and saw her father smiling.

CHAPTER 2

That night, Molly had a strange, disturbing dream about Romey and Rairarubia. In the morning, she couldn't remember much, only that the dream left her feeling kind of funny inside. Not funny ha-ha, but funny weird-like. She didn't know how to describe it. But she couldn't seem to get Rairarubia or Romey out of her mind after she woke up.

Since it was Saturday, Molly got to sleep late. She was still in bed trying to remember her dream when her father stuck his head in her room and reminded her she had promised to help clean out the garage for her school's rummage sale.

After a couple of hours of sorting through dusty boxes and garage junk, Molly decided she and her dad needed a break. The strange feelings from her dream still with her, Molly thought that maybe if they continued the story she might remember her dream and shake off her odd feelings.

"Dad, let's get back to Romey."

"Romey? Romey who?" Her father continued moving some boxes around.

"Come on, dad! You know!" Molly threw a wet cleaning rag she was using and hit his arm with a smack.

"Oh, *that* Romey," he threw the rag back at her, but she ducked.

"Come on, or I'm going to quit helping you clean." She plunked down on her old Red Racer wagon she never played with anymore and scooted it toward her dad.

"Hey, no help, no story. Anyway, you're supposed to make it up *with* me, remember?"

"Yeah, but come on. At least finish the part about Romey falling through the snow."

"What a pest! Okay, but you've got to help me out."

Molly watched him as he lifted a big box and put it on a shelf. She could tell he was thinking up more story. Then he opened a small, three-step ladder and sat on the top.

"Let's see, now. Romey was sliding down…"

"Really fast—like in a circling slide at the Water World Park."

"Exactly. Well, just when Romey thought she'd never stop sliding…"

Romey found herself free falling through space.

"Aheee!" she yelled, feeling her stomach being left behind.

Falling faster and faster, she watched as the little ribbon of a river below got wider and wider, the lake closer and closer. Was this the end?

Then Romey remembered her feathered cape. Maybe, just maybe…

Holding tight to each end of her feathered cape, Romey stretched out both arms. Her falling began to slow into a gentle glide. Then she discovered by tilting her body and arms a little this way or that way she could maneuver and turn. Soon she was soaring around like a hang glider.

"I'm flying!" she cried out. "I'm really flying!"

Enjoying her discovery, Romey circled around and around, dipping, gliding, rising, diving. So this was what it was like to fly like a bird! Things looked so different.

Before long, her arms tired. She didn't want to, but realized she'd better come down. Reluctantly, she began circling closer and closer to the ground that came toward her very fast—too fast. Fearing she might get hurt if she hit land, she aimed for the lake.

Just moments before she hit water, Romey shook off her feathered cape, took a deep breath, held her nose, and plunged into the lake. Her body felt a thousand pin-like stings as she sank into the cold water. Quickly, she kicked and pulled her way to the surface.

The freezing water, along with arms tired from flying, made swimming difficult. And her shoes and clothes weighed her down. Realizing she could never make it to shore with them on, Romey struggled and finally managed to remove her shoes and overalls, which soon sank from sight.

Looking around, Romey wasn't sure which way to swim. Every direction toward shore looked about equal. So she just began swimming toward land.

At first, Romey wondered where she had learned to swim. But that only reminded her she knew nothing about her past before the big bird. So she just swam. For a while she would do the breast stroke, then the crawl, then a side stroke. To rest, she did a type of back stroke. But land didn't seem to be getting any closer. She shivered from the cold and felt numb all over. Her vision became blurred.

"Keep going. You can do it, Romey."

Whose voice was that? Was it her own? She didn't know anymore. She didn't care. She just kept stroking, kicking, stroking, kicking, feeling nothing, seeing nothing. But soon she could no longer move, feeling cold and tired and sleepy.

Then she sank slowly into the cold depths of the lake.

Sometime later, Romey awoke with a start. She was lying by a small fire, and someone had put a blanket over her. She sat up and realized that she was no longer in the lake, but in a cave.

"Hey! What happened? Where am I?" she asked aloud. She looked around. No one was in sight.

Even though she was puzzled by what had happened, Romey's growling stomach felt more of a need for food than answers. She couldn't remember the last time she had eaten.

With just her thought of food, a plate of fruit, cheese, and bread appeared by the fire. Had it been there before? She didn't think so. But she was too hungry to care. She picked up a bright red apple and looked it over carefully. It looked good, so she took a small bite. Delicious! She ate more, then ate some cheese, then some bread, some grapes, and soon the plate was empty.

"That's better. But now I'm thirsty," she thought to herself.

As soon as she thought it, a large cup of cold water appeared next to the plate which was full of food once more.

Romey jumped back against the cave wall.

"Yikes and spikes! What's going on here? I know that wasn't there before," she said aloud.

"Did you rest well, my dear?" a soft voice asked from within the dark. It was a strange voice, neither earthly nor unearthly, old nor young, male nor female, high nor low.

Startled, Romey squinted beyond the fire for the person behind the voice. "Who are you? Where am? How did I get here? The last thing I remember I …"

"'Everything in good time, Romey. Don't be impatient. And don't be afraid," the soothing voice said.

"I'm not afraid." When she said it, Romey realized it was true.

"I'm sure you are not," replied the voice. "That's why you are here."

Romey stood up, surprised to notice she was now wearing a long white robe with a red ribbon around the waist. The gold necklace and pendant still hung about her neck.

"How do you know my name? Where are you? Why don't you show yourself?"

"You will see me when the time comes, if you are the chosen one—and if you pass the tests."

"Chosen one? Tests? What kind of tests? And where are my own clothes?"

"One of the tests will be to learn patience. If, as you say, you are not afraid, then trust me."

"I'm not afraid, but if you want my trust, then you'll have to earn it. Why should I trust you? You don't even show yourself."

"Ah, well spoken, Romey. You are right. Trust should be earned, and then, of course, respected. Neither should it be given away too freely. Think a moment. Have you been harmed in any way?"

"No."

"Look there, by the fire."

Romey looked and saw her clothes neatly laid out, including her shoes and overall jeans. But she also knew they hadn't been there until she'd been told to look.

"Have I threatened you in any way?" asked the voice.

"No." Then she added, "Not yet, anyway."

"Have I not brought you in safely from your ordeal with the giant bird, your plunge into the lake? Have I not warmed you, fed you, dressed you in dry clothes?"

"How do you know about the bird? And how did I get here? I remember swimming, the cold ..." Romey's curiosity was totally in motion now.

"I know many things, Romey, and much of it I'd like to share with you. But you must trust me. If you don't, you are free to leave now. But then neither of us will ever know if you are the chosen one."

"I don't know anything about a chosen one. I don't even know where I come from. I can't remember anything before the bird captured me. I don't understand what any of this is about." Romey's confusion showed in her voice.

"Listen, Romey. There is an old story about a man who left his young daughter alone while he was gone for a few days. When he returned, his house was burned nearly to ruins. He found in the ashes what he believed to be the charred body of his daughter. He fell to his knees and wept and wept. After his child's burial, he kept a small toy of hers on a chain around his neck.

"But the truth was his daughter had not been burned with the house. She had been kidnapped by bandits. But she escaped a year later. When she arrived at her father's house late one night, she knocked at the door. Her father demanded to know who it was. She told him, 'I am your daughter.' But the father, holding the toy on the chain around his neck, wept and told her to go away, that his daughter was dead. She tried to convince him, but he would not believe her. The daughter left and the father lost her forever."

"The father was stupid," Romey replied, still not understanding why she was being told the story.

"Truth knocked on the father's door, but he would not let it in. The point is, Romey, that when we believe something to be the only truth and hold fast to it, we cannot be open to new ideas or other views."

"But what has this to do with me? Am I the daughter in the story?" Romey hoped not. The idea of a father turning her away made her sad.

"No, Romey. I was only speaking in symbols. But you *are* free of attachments, are you not? And you have shown intelligence and bravery in the face of danger." Then the voice added, "More importantly, you wear the necklace."

Romey fingered the medallion around her neck and wondered why the voice thought it was so important.

"We believe you are the chosen one. Are you open to letting the truth in? We believe you are. You are strong and have the capacity to liberate yourself and the good within others. We are willing to teach you what you need to know. Are you willing to learn?"

As the voice spoke, an opening from the cave suddenly appeared with a soft swish. Romey could see the blue sky, green trees outside, the lake in the distance. Her chance to get away stood open before her.

The voice spoke again. "Leave now, or trust me and stay for the tests. But you must make your choice now."

Romey stood looking at the exit from the cave. What to do? What did the voice mean by the chosen one? What would the tests be like? What if she was being tricked? Was the person behind the voice evil or good? What would she be taught? If she stayed, who knows what might happen to her? Would she find out who she was? Was there a purpose behind all this?

Molly's father stopped to look at his watch. "Uh, oh! Look at the time, kiddo. "

"Well, don't stop there, dad. Go on," Molly urged.

"You've got to get ready for your piano lesson. Look at us. We're a mess." He got off the ladder and brushed dust and dirt from his sleeves and jeans. "And don't forget, your mom's taking you shopping this afternoon."

"Aw, come on, dad!" Molly protested. "First tell me what Romey decides to do."

"I think you can guess," her father winked a smile. He brushed some pieces of dirt from Molly's shoulders and back.

"No. Come on, please tell me." Molly felt herself being gently pulled from her wagon and led into the house.

"What would you do if you were Romey?"

"But I'm not Romey." As soon as Molly said the words, she felt her face grow warm, dozens of butterflies fluttered in her stomach, and her legs felt like sponges. She shivered and seemed far away, barely hearing her father's words.

"Then we'll just have to wait and see, won't we?"

CHAPTER 3

Molly's piano lesson didn't go very well. Her mind couldn't let go of Romey. And even that afternoon, when her mother took her shopping for new clothes, Molly still carried disturbing feelings she couldn't explain. She knew it showed when her mother asked if Molly felt okay. That made Molly feel even worse, because she loved going shopping and being with her mother. Emergencies at the clinic often canceled plans she and her mother made.

For some reason, Molly didn't tell her parents about her strange feelings. Mostly, she didn't know how. How could she explain that she felt like she was in two places at once and no place at all? How could she tell them that all she could think about was Rairarubia. It was just a made-up story! It didn't make sense.

But she had to talk about it to someone, so that evening she called her best friend, Netty.

"It's really weird, Netty. I can't even begin to explain it, but something strange is happening to me."

"Just because of this story you and your dad made up? What d'ya call it? Rare-a-rubadub?" Netty laughed and didn't sound sympathetic enough for Molly. But that was Netty. She had little patience for things she didn't understand.

"Rairarubia. Anyway, I know it sounds weirdo, but it's like—it's like my mind is being taken over by Romey. I don't want to think about her, but I do anyway. And when my dad starts telling the story, well, sometimes it feels like I already know what's going to happen. But I don't. I mean, not really. Know what I mean?"

"No."

"Well, thanks a lot, friend." Molly envisioned Netty sitting cross-legged on the floor, her red hair done in pig tails, twirling the telephone cord around her fingers.

"Well, what d'ya expect, Molly? How can I know what you're talking about when you can't even explain it. You're probably coming down with the flu that's going around."

"That's what my mom thinks. But I don't think so. It's not a sick body feeling. It's—it's like nerves or something."

"You're too young to have a nervous breakdown."

"Oh, Netty! Just—just forget it. I'll see you at school Monday."

Calling Netty hadn't helped. And the more she tried not to think about Romey, the more she did.

She decided she had to get her dad to tell more of the story, maybe even finish it so she could feel normal again.

Most nights at Molly's bedtime, her parents sat on her bed with her and together they read a chapter from a book. One night her mother would read, the next night her father. The routine was as comfortable and familiar as her room. Bookshelves on one wall contained an assortment of things besides books: stuffed animals she had collected over the years, different sized boxes containing various games and puzzles, her own stereo system. Another wall had pictures of friends, mostly Netty, posters from places she had been, a school calendar, and several drawings and paintings that Molly had done. Outside her window grew a Japanese maple tree she had helped plant just last year.

Tonight, however, her mother had been called into the clinic on some emergency. That gave Molly an idea.

"Dad, instead of reading tonight, let's get back to Rairarubia."

"Hmm, I don't know. I'm kinda' anxious to see what's going to happen to Charles Wallace."

"Me, too. And so is mom. But it wouldn't be fair to her if we read *A Wrinkle in Time* tonight. So let's get back to Romey. That way mom won't miss any of the book."

"Boy, kiddo, you're really getting into our little make-believe world, aren't you? Well, I guess in fairness to your mother we should skip the book tonight. So, where were we?"

"Come on. You know. Romey had to decide if she was going to leave the cave or trust the voice and take some tests to see if she's the chosen one."

"Right. Well, what do you think she decides to do?"

"I think she'll stay and trust the voice."

"Why?"

"Because it'll make a more interesting story." But Molly secretly felt it was more than that. Exactly what she wasn't sure.

"You think so, huh? Well, then, I guess we'd better find out."

Molly waited while her father scratched his chin and stared into space. After a moment, he continued, "So, Romey tells the hidden voice her decision is to stay ..."

"Good. So be it," the hidden voice answered. "Let the tests begin."

And with those words the cave opening disappeared, just vanished before her eyes. Now she was in the dark except for the light from the small fire. For a moment, Romey wondered if she had made the right choice. Was she trapped now?

"Close your eyes, Romey, and no matter what you feel or hear, don't open them until I tell you. If you do, you will go blind."

"Blind? Really?" Romey wonder if the voice was trying to scare her.

20

"Yes." The voice was convincing.

"Why do you want me to close my eyes?"

"This is the first test of trust," replied the voice.

So Romey closed her eyes. Soon she felt as if the ground were moving and it made her a little dizzy. Then she heard a noise like a strong wind whooshing through the forest. Her skin felt damp, then warm. Even with her eyes closed she could tell there was a brilliant light somewhere.

Was she moving? She wasn't sure. She wanted so much to open her eyes, but if this was a test of trust, she told herself, then she was going to do what she had been told.

She lost track of time. It could have been seconds, minutes, but it felt like hours. Finally, a woman's soft voice said, "You may open your eyes now, Romey."

At first she couldn't see anything. The bright light forced her to squint while adjusting to it. But gradually things fell into focus.

Romey stood stunned by where she was and what she saw. She was on the edge of a wooden bridge that crossed a wide moat surrounding the most magnificent castle anyone could ever imagine. The heavy wooden double doors on the other side of the bridge rose at least twenty feet. A huge letter **R** made up of red jewels, rubies she thought, sat above the doorway.

"Is this for real or have I gone bonkers?" Romey asked, but received no answer.

Rounded towers extended upward on either side of the doors. Romey almost fell over backwards looking up at the tall, red, coned-shaped tops where flags, each with a red **R** on a white background, unfurled lazily in the breeze. Lower than the towers by half, the castle walls sparkled with precious stones of red, yellow, green, and blue embedded in them. The walls stretched more than half a mile on both sides of the towers.

"Where am I?" Romey asked the voice.

"Rairarubia Castle, the center of the Land of Rair-arubia."

Romey looked around when she heard the voice, but no one was there.

"Where are you? Why won't you let me see you?"

"All in good time. Enter, Romey, don't be afraid," the voice told her.

Romey hesitated a moment, then began crossing the bridge. It was then she noticed that she was no longer in the white robe, but dressed in clothes she had never seen before.

"Wait a minute! How the … ?"

She examined herself. She now wore a plain, soft, dark-blue blouse and matching pants tucked into knee-high boots made of a soft brown leather. A light blue sash about two inches wide was tied around her waist, the two ends hanging loose a few inches. She still wore the medallion.

"This is so weird." Amazed, she tried to look more closely at what she was wearing.

"There's no time for that, Romey. You must enter the castle now," the voice reminded.

"Okay, okay, I'm going."

As she crossed the bridge to the castle entrance, she noticed two huge guards dressed in red on either side of the doorway. They each wore a knife and a sword and held a long, sharp-looking spear.

She stopped and looked down from the bridge at the dirty water below just as an alligator-like animal pulled itself up on the bank.

"Uh-oh. What have I gotten myself into? What if these guards won't let me in?" she thought to herself.

The voice seemed to read her mind. "Don't worry, Romey. You will see much, but no one will see you. To them, you don't exist. Not yet."

"Not yet? What does that mean, 'not yet'?"

Romey received no answer.

She paused a moment, reminding herself this was a

test, took a deep breath, and then approached the doorway. The guards paid no attention to her. She walked between them as though she were invisible.

Feeling bold, she couldn't resist. She went back and stood in front of one of the guards and made a face. Nothing happened, which made her even more daring.

"Nyeah, nyeah, nyeah, nyeah," she said to the guard, making silly faces. He didn't move. Didn't he see her?

Romey stood in front of another guard with her hands on her hips and shouted, "Hey, big guy! If you can't guard any better than this, you better get a new job!"

Then the voice spoke, "That's enough, Romey. Let it be sufficient that he can't see you."

"Okay, okay, just having a little fun."

Once through the huge doorway, Romey came upon the open courtyard. She did not like what her eyes and nose were forced to take in. It looked and smelled like the dirtiest, poorest place in the world. Some people were moving about as if afraid, their heads hanging down, looking sad and defeated. She noticed several fights taking place, one over a piece of clothing, another over a torn loaf of bread.

Two uniformed men were laughing and kicking someone lying on the ground. Several beggars in tattered clothes held out their hands asking others for food. Romey saw a woman steal something from another person's basket. Some children threw rocks at a yelping dog. No one seemed happy. Just the mood of the place felt ugly.

Then the ground shook. The sound of horses' hooves on the stone courtyard suddenly caused everyone to freeze with fear. Then people started running about and hiding. Those who couldn't get away cleared a path for a dozen riders who entered on magnificent horses. The men, well dressed from head to foot in black leather, wore swords at their sides. Some had maces tied to their saddles, others carried lances and shields.

One very large man rode in front of the group and

stared straight ahead. That he was their leader was easy to tell. A red cape fell from his shoulders and partly covered a saddle laden with twinkling jewels of various sizes and shapes.

Romey was wondering who he was when the voice again seemed to know her thoughts.

"He is Mammoth. At present, he rules Rairarubia."

"From the looks of things, I'd say he's not doing a very good job of ruling. With all the jewels I see stuck in the walls, this place should be rich." Romey shook her head. "Why are you showing me all this?"

"If you are the chosen one, it will be your duty to change all this for the better."

"My duty? Me? Why me? I'm just a girl. I don't even know where I come from. What even makes you think I'm this—this chosen one?"

"Because you wear the golden medallion around your neck."

"What? This old thing? I found it in a bird's nest!"

"Still, you wear it."

"But ..."

"You must go now, Romey. Your invisibility is fading. The tests must begin."

"Wait! I ..."

But before Romey could finish, a cloud surrounded her. The ground began moving and she felt that dizziness again, that same wind, the damp, the brilliant light. She heard a swishing noise and then the mist cleared.

No longer in Rairarubia Castle, Romey stood in the middle of a large grassy field near rolling hills dotted with clumps of trees.

"Weirdo. I mean *really* weirdo," she spoke half aloud.

"You can say that again," said a voice behind her.

Romey, startled, turned quickly and found a boy about her age standing with his legs apart and hands resting on his hips. A thick lock of red hair fell over his forehead, almost covering one of his large, dark eyes. Compared to what she had seen in Rairarubia, he had a friendly face.

"Well, I guess I'm not invisible to you. So, who are you?" Romey asked, noticing that he was dressed in the same type of clothes as she, but stood slightly taller.

"I have the same question. Just who are *you*?" the boy asked.

"I asked first." Romey faced the boy, legs apart and hands on her hips, looking a little defiant. At least this voice had a body.

The boy looked her over for a few moments. Then, with a broad smile, he answered.

"Name's Sam. And yours?" He walked toward Romey and held out his hand.

"Sam," Romey repeated. She looked Sam over as he had done her before telling him her name. Then she took his extended hand and they both gripped tight as they shook.

"Whoosits! You have a strong hand," Sam said, impressed.

Romey seemed to ignore the compliment, looked around, then asked, "Are you here to be tested, too?"

"Yes, but I don't know what kind of test, do you?" Sam's eyes also searched around.

"No." Romey hesitated a moment, not certain she should confide in Sam. Then she decided she could. "I don't even know why or how I got here. And everything keeps changing."

Seeing nothing but green rolling hills and some clumps of trees sprinkled here and there, she sat down cross-legged and began pulling absently on her necklace.

Sam sat down facing her. "Looks like you lost all the jewels in your necklace."

Romey looked at the medallion absently. She didn't see any reason to reply to such an obvious statement.

They sat quietly for a while, each occasionally looking about or at each other. Then Sam broke the silence.

"Well, to be honest, Romey, I don't know why or how I got here either. I don't even know where I come from. It's almost like I have amnesia or something. I seem to remember falling … and a cave. Something about taking some tests. Then all of a sudden I was in some terrible place called Rairarubia Castle." Sam's voice faded with his last words.

"You, too? So was I."

"Really? Whoosits. This gets more confusing all the time."

Sam's words made Romey feel a little better, less alone. "I know what you mean. Almost the same thing happened to me, but the memory is fading. There was this big bird—and I fell—yes, a cave—tests—and the castle in Rairarubia. Where exactly *is* Rairarubia, anyway? Do you know?" Romey looked at Sam.

Sam shrugged his shoulders. "Beats me, I don't know anything except I'm supposed to take some tests of some kind to prove I'm worthy of something, but I don't even know what the something is. But I'll tell you one thing, I'd sure like to know what's going on."

Romey sympathized with Sam's agitation.

"All in good time," the soft woman's voice stated, still hidden.

Both Romey and Sam jumped up, looking about for the source of the words.

"Don't bother looking for me," the voice said with a hint of a laugh. "It's time for the first test to begin. Are you both ready?"

"What's the test?" Romey asked, still looking around.

"A test of what, exactly?" Sam wanted to know.

"A test of yourselves, as you will now see. If you pass this test, you will be eligible for the next," the voice answered.

"And if we fail?" Romey asked the air around them.

"Concentrate on passing, Romey, not on failing," the

voice told her.

"I'd like to know more about what's going on here. Why can't you tell us?"

"Yeah, what's all this about?" Sam injected in an annoyed tone to match Romey's.

"The test. First, the test … the test …" The words became a fading echo.

For a moment, Romey and Sam stood in silence. Then in exasperation, Romey turned in a slow circle, yelling to the disappeared voice, "So where's the test? What are we supposed to do? I don't know what you want!"

There was no answer.

The two expectantly stood there for a moment but nothing happened. Finally, Romey said, "Well, I'm not going to just stand here forever. This is stupid. It's getting hot. I'm heading for that bunch of trees over there."

"I'm with you," Sam agreed, and they started walking.

After a few steps, the ground started to tremble slightly, then roll slowly, then shake vigorously with a rumbling sound. Suddenly, Romey and Sam were knocked to their hands and knees as the earth waved and tilted violently. With a loud, fearful tearing noise, the earth split apart. A wide, deep gap began opening in the ground just inches in front of them.

"Whirling whoosits!" Sam called out. "What in the name of…?"

Before he could finish, both he and Romey went sliding feet first toward the wide-growing split. Romey's lower body slipped over the ledge as Sam, digging his fingers of one hand into the ground, grabbed one of Romey's arms and held on to her. Then, just as suddenly as it started, all became quiet and still again.

Sam pulled at Romey's arm with all his strength as he and Romey each managed to clutch earth with their free hand and gradually claw and elbow away from the deep break in the earth.

Romey and Sam quickly crawled away on all fours from the edge of the new rip in the ground. The broad gap seemed to run for miles in both directions with no bottom in sight.

"Yikes and spikes! For a minute I thought the rip wanted me for dinner. Thanks, Sam."

"What in the name of whirling whoosits was that all about?" Sam asked, ignoring her thanks.

"I thought we were goners." Romey crawled farther away from the rip.

"This is supposed to be a test?" Sam wondered, now standing up. He offered Romey his hand to help her up. She ignored his gesture and got up by herself.

"Well, I'm not staying here," Romey said, "and I'm getting away from this overgrown gully as fast as I can." She started in the opposite direction of the new split.

"Hey, wait for me. Let's work together on this test thing," Sam said, catching up with Romey.

They walked away from the crevice for a while not saying anything. Then Romey slowed down and turned to Sam.

"You don't think that—that earthquake, or whatever it was, could be part of the test, do you?"

"What do you mean? How could it be part of the test?"

"Well, for one thing, we don't know what the test is. Maybe they—the voice—whoever—wanted to see how we'd react to the ground opening up like that. Maybe to see what we'd do. How we'd act as a, you know, team."

"Hmm; I dunno." Sam thought for a moment. "But if so, why? What's the point?"

Romey shrugged her shoulders. She wished she knew what the point was, what the test was, what she was doing here, where she came from, where Sam came from, what was expected of her in Rairarubia. Her brain felt like a hundred bees buzzing inside trying to get out.

"Say," Sam interrupted her beehive, "maybe . . . ."

"What?"

"Naw, it sounds too weird."

"Hey, are you kidding? Weird is the *only* word for what's going on. What were you going to say?" Romey was open to almost any explanation.

"Well, maybe the earth splitting stuff was meant to make us go in this direction. I mean, there we were, not knowing what to expect and—whoosits—we're cut off from one direction. The way we're headed is our only choice, the way they must want us to go."

"Ha! A nice voice telling us to turn around would have been a lot easier!"

But then Romey thought about what Sam suggested. "You might be right, but we could have decided to go along the split in either direction, left or right, instead of this way," Romey reasoned.

"True, but I don't think so, the more I think about it. We got jarred pretty strong. The split could have gotten bigger; we could've fallen in. It was natural to move away from the ledge rather than follow it. I think they wanted to see how we'd react together at the unexpected *and* send us a directional message." Sam sounded more convinced he was right the more he talked.

"Maybe, but ..." Romey stopped abruptly and pointed ahead. Sam stopped and saw it, too.

"Sam, I think you just might be right."

Molly's father was quiet for too long to suit her.

"Well, what did they see, daddy?"

"Ah, now that's a good question."

"So answer it!"

"I can't. I don't know myself. Anyway, it's past your bedtime."

"Ah, come on, dad, just tell me what they saw."

"Next time. You think about it as you fall asleep and give me some ideas for next time. Remember, you're supposed to be helping me with this story."

"I'll never fall asleep now. I need to know. Oh, please." But Molly knew it was no use.

Her father smiled, kissed her on the forehead, and turned out the bedroom light.

As he left her room, Molly called after him, "Meany!"

"I love you, too. 'Night, kiddo. Sleep well."

But Molly didn't sleep well. At one time during the night, she even thought she heard her name being called, but decided she must be dreaming.

CHAPTER 4

School on Monday was not easy. Molly thought maybe she was going crazy. Rairarubia constantly filled her mind. She kept thinking about Romey and Sam and seeing the letter R in her head. Twice, she got called on by the teacher to answer a question, but Molly had no idea what the questions had been.

During lunch, she tried again to explain to Netty what was going on in her mind, but Netty thought she was just being stupid.

"Your problem's simple," Netty told her. "Just end the story. Have Sam and Romey get married and live happily ever after."

"You just don't understand," Molly told her. But Molly didn't understand what was happening either.

On Tuesday, Molly had a sore throat and a headache. So did her father. Her mother had insisted that Molly stay home and that she and her father get lots of rest and drink plenty of liquids. "I don't need you two as patients at the clinic," she told them when she left for work.

At mid-morning, Molly, still in her pajamas, sat in bed trying unsuccessfully to read when her father stuck his head in her room. "How you feeling, kiddo?"

"Yuk. My eyes hurt to read. And my mind wanders." She dropped her book on the floor.

"Yeah, me, too. I can't work very well today." He sat next to her and felt her forehead. "Hey, you're pretty warm."

"Yeah. I feel hot, then I feel cold." Molly shivered and pulled her bed covers up to her chin.

"Maybe you need a nap." He felt her warm forehead.

"Huh-uh. Tell me more about Romey and Sam." As bad as she felt, Molly still had Rairarubia on her mind

"Between blowing my nose and coughing, I don't know if I can," he told her. "And my head feels too thick and dull for creativity."

"Just try, please, just a little more."

"Lordy, what a pest." Molly saw him smile weakly. "OK. Maybe a little bit. Where were we? Oh, yes ..."

Sam looked where Romey was pointing. In the distance they saw a tall, dark-green hedge that seemed to run for miles in both directions.

As they approached the wall of green, it seemed to get taller with every step. Soon they stood in front of a thick growth of tangled bushes, vines, and shrubbery that rose at least three times as tall as they.

"What now?" Sam wondered aloud.

Romey tried to peer through the hedge, but the thick branches scratched her arms as she tried to spread them apart.

"Well, we can't get through here," Romey said, rubbing her itchy arms.

"Or go over it," Sam said standing back and looking upward.

"Look, you go to the left, and I'll go to the right for a bit. The first one to see a way through, let out a yell," suggested Romey.

"OK," Sam agreed, "but let's don't separate by too much. Keep in sight."

They split up, each heading in the opposite direction looking for some kind of opening. Both looked back periodically making certain they could still see the other. They even got on their hands and knees to look through the dense tangle of thick branches and roots for anything that looked like a way through. But after a time, they found nothing.

"This is useless," Sam yelled, throwing his hands up in the air and squatting down on the grass.

Romey felt relieved Sam was the first to give up, because she was ready to say the same thing. But then she noticed something partially hidden behind tangled vines.

"Sam, come here. I may have found something."

By the time Sam reached her, Romey had pulled away some of the twigs and branches that weren't too thick for her to bend and snap.

"What is it? Did you find an opening?" Sam saw what Romey was trying to get at.

"I can't tell what it is. I think so. Help me pull some of this brush away."

Putting up with scratched arms and cut fingers, the pair finally revealed a small wooden door that had become hidden by overgrown brush. The old door was plain except for a big door knob in the center. Set inside the knob's center was an oval-shaped ruby that glittered brightly.

"Whoosits! Would you look at that!" Sam reached out and touched the door knob.

"OOWWEE!" He leaped back, grabbed his hand, and jumped up and down.

"What happened?" Romey almost laughed at the way Sam had jumped and yelled, but hoped he wasn't really hurt.

"Whirling whoosits! That thing gave me a shock. Don't touch it," Sam warned.

Romey didn't want to experience what Sam had, but she wondered how they were going to get through the door. Cautiously, and half in jest, she knocked on the door. Sam smirked at her as if she were crazy.

"Well, it's worth a try," she said to his look.

"Who's there?" the door asked.

Romey and Sam looked at each other, startled.

"Uh, we are—us—Romey and Sam," Romey told the door.

"What do you want?" the door demanded.

"What do you think we want?" Sam said still holding his stinging hand. "We want in."

"To gain entry, you must answer three riddles."

"What three riddles?" Romey questioned.

"The Riddles of the Door. Only those who know the answers to the three riddles are permitted to take the class verte."

Romey and Sam gave each other a puzzled look and together asked, "Class verte?"

"This is the doorway to the class verte, the source of knowledge about all plant and animal life. Only those who have passed the test of bravery and quick wit get this far. To get this far shows you possess bravery and intelligence. If you can answer the Riddles of the Door, you will be allowed to enter your class verte training."

"So what are these riddles?" Sam still sounded annoyed at being shocked.

"Only one of you may answer. Riddle number one: What flies forever, and rests never?"

Sam shrugged his shoulders and looked at Romey with a silly face that let her know he didn't care for riddles.

Romey, frowned in thinking, then smiled.

"The wind."

"Correct," the door told her.

Sam's face lit up in surprise.

"Riddle number two: The strongest man cannot stand against me. I can knock him down, yet I do not hurt him. And he feels better because I have knocked him down. What am I?"

Again Sam shrugged and looked at Romey who closed her eyes in thought. Sam thought she was about to give up when she replied, "Sleep."

"Correct again," spoke the door.

"Hey, go Romey," Sam said, "very impressive, very impressive."

The door went on. "Now, riddle number three: The more you feed it, the more it will grow high. But if you give it water, then it will quickly die."

"Oh, I know that one," Sam said excitedly.

"Fire," Romey quickly told the door, remembering only one was allowed to answer.

"Correct," the door said once again.

"Hey, I knew that," Sam said a bit put out. "You never gave me a chance to answer."

Romey ignored him and reached for the door knob. She hesitated a moment, wondering if she would get a shock. Then she grabbed it and turned.

Instead of a shock, the oval ruby in the door knob fell into her hand.

"Hey, look a this." Romey held the stone out for Sam to see.

"Pretty little thing." Sam picked it up and turned it over and over in his fingers. "But what's it for? Think there's any connection with all this?"

"I don't know. It probably just came loose by accident."

Sam handed the ruby back to Romey. As she reached for it, the medallion fell from her shirt and swung slightly back and forth, catching Sam's eye.

"Whoosits!" Sam said. "Gimme that thing again."

Taking the ruby from Romey, he took hold of the medallion around her neck and snapped the ruby in the empty oval-shaped recess. "Look at that! It fits."

No sooner had he said those words, when the door swung open. The pair jumped back, staring in disbelief. They looked at each other, both with open mouths. Then Romey started toward the door.

"Guess there's no doubt about what we're to do next."

Sam hesitated a second, then quickly caught up with her. "Right with you."

For the first few steps inside they could see nothing but a brightness, but they kept walking. Then there was a swishing noise behind them and they turned to see the door close up again.

"Oh, oh," Sam muttered, looking warily at Romey. But then the brightness began to fade, and what they saw before them was of more interest than the closing behind.

"Wonderful whirling whoosits!" Sam uttered.

Romey's mouth dropped open. She couldn't find the right words.

Like a kaleidoscope, vivid colors on a background of green flashed everywhere she looked. Flowers of every imaginable shade of red, blue, green, yellow, and white spread out before them. Plants, small and tall, grew all around. Tall trees loomed in the background. Together, the view looked like a sparkling mixture of flower garden, forest, and jungle.

When Romey turned to Sam, she saw his clothes had turned green and so had hers.

"You found the ruby. Welcome."

The pair let out a startled noise as they jumped and turned to face the voice. This time there was a body to go with it.

"Don't be frightened. My name is Bovert. I will be your teacher and guide while you are here."

Bovert had on a green outfit like theirs, but his sash was a much deeper green. Pushed back on his curly blond hair sat a small green cap with the letter **R** sewn on front. His friendly face and green eyes held a warm smile, showing white, even teeth. He was thin, which made him look taller than his six feet. In his arms he held what appeared at first to be a large cat, but on second look was a baby leopard. Its eyes seemed just sleepy slits, but both Romey and Sam realized the animal was watching them closely. Bovert scratched the cat between its ears, but he, too, was sizing up the new arrivals.

"Where are we?" Sam wanted to know.

"Teach us what?" Romey asked at the same time.

Bovert smiled more broadly. "To answer Sam's question ..."

"How do you know my name?" Sam interrupted.

"You're in the class verte training section, a remote part of Rairarubia," Bovert went on, ignoring Sam's question. "As I said, I'm Bovert, your teacher and guide. You are my pupils for a time."

"Teacher of what exactly? I don't mean to be rude," Romey said, "but everybody seems to be stalling me when it comes to answers."

Bovert nodded his head, smiling. "Good. You're both full of questions. You'll make interesting students. As to what you will learn, that's up to you. Look around. Listen."

The three were quiet. But all around them came various animal sounds from deep bellowing to light chirping. They couldn't see all the animals making the sounds, but they knew there were hearing many varieties of life.

"Come," Bovert said quietly, placing the small leopard on the ground and walking toward the dense forest. The cat quickly lost itself among the vegetation.

"Where?" Romey asked, not moving.

"Come, please," he said, smiling back as he moved forward.

Something about Bovert's whole manner caused Romey to trust him. She shrugged her shoulders and followed Bovert. She had come this far on trust, why not farther?

"Hey, wait for me," Sam blustered out and followed along.

After a few steps, the three stopped at the edge of a canyon precipice. Romey and Sam felt as if they were standing on the edge of the world. Far below and across from them a wide, white-water river ran swiftly through a narrow canyon. Further below, it funneled into a waterfall that emptied into a deep blue lake. Around the lake, fields of multi-colored flowers spread out toward green rolling hills spotted with tall, thickly leafed trees. Small and large animals grazed in peaceful contentment. Birds of all types fluttered in the trees or circled around the fields and lake. Behind the curved hills rose jagged mountains covered with snow.

"Whoosit!"

Romey asked, "This is all part of Rairarubia?"

"A small part," replied Bovert.

As they took in the wondrous sights of nature, Bovert suddenly raised one arm and waved it across the sky. Instantly, the view changed. Most of the trees were now cut down. Only a few scraggly ones could be seen. The green of the hills was now brown and parched. The flowered fields had turned to swamp marsh. A low, thick, yellowish-gray haze blocked sight of the mountains. Below, the river was now just a few puddles here and there. Dead animals and bones lay near the small stagnant pools of water that once was the lake. There was no sign or sounds of life.

"What happened?" Romey cried. "What did you do?"

Sam was speechless for once.

"You see a possible future," Bovert said solemnly. "This is why it is important for you to learn well while you are here."

"Learn what?" Sam asked, staring out at the sad sight.

"How this future Rairarubia might be avoided," Bovert replied. "You are here to learn how to live in nature and how to treat nature. You will learn how to survive among animals, how to live off the land, what is good to eat, what is not, what to fear, what not to fear. You will learn that you are part of nature, not just living in it. You will learn what to touch and what not to touch. You will learn to respect what nature has to offer you and your part in it. You will, if you are able, enter the very heart of nature—you will learn to *be* nature."

Bovert raised his arm and waved it once more. There again lay their first glimpse of the land of Rairarubia.

"Come, let the lessons begin," Bovert said and walked into the green growth. Soon the three of them disappeared into the thick, dark green landscape.

Molly's dad was silent for a while, causing Molly to ask, "What's it like? In where they went? Is it nice or scary? Don't stop now."

"Sorry, kiddo, but my voice is giving out, or hadn't you noticed. That's all for now."

Molly could see her dad wasn't feeling well, so she didn't push him this time. Besides, she didn't feel very well either.

Almost as soon as her father left, Molly fell into a troublesome, sweaty sleep and dreamt she was trying to find Romey in a shoulder high garden of thorny bushes and wild animal cries.

CHAPTER 5

The next day, her father felt better, but Molly never felt more terrible in her life. Every part of her body ached. She didn't want to eat or drink. Her fever ran high and she knew it worried her parents, who were doing everything they could to help Molly fight off the illness. It was the flu, her mother said.

Then, as her fever worsened, Molly fell in and out of consciousness. Sometimes she floated, drifting along in a mindless air stream. She could not control her mind or body. She would feel hot and wet, then shiver in a cold blackness. Sometimes she wasn't sure were she was.

"We're right here, honey." She knew her parents sat close by her bed. Still, they seemed so far away.

"Can't we do anything?"

Was that her father?

"We'll just have to wait now."

"Mommy? Are you holding my hand?" Molly's body felt heavy, then light, floating away . . . drifting . . . into nature . . . not just in it . . . a part of it . . . a part of nature . . . colorful flowers . . . look up at the birds . . . be a bird . . . look down at the snake . . . be a snake . . . hot here in nature . . . here, take my hand . . . someone's talking . . . shhh . . . listen . . . "You will learn that you are part of nature . . . to *be* nature . . . ."

Who's that? Bovert, is that you standing there? Is

this Rairarubia? Long shafts of light from above split through the tall, jagged rows of alders, cedars, and fir trees. The air was quiet and hazy. The forest floor they walked on ...*they* ? ... who was she with? ... was made of soft mounds of earth and moss created from thousands of years of fallen trees.

"We are stepping on the ancient litter of pine needles, broken twigs, and bark," he told them. Buried deep beneath them were the roots and pieces of trees and plants no one living had ever seen. Now they formed the present surface of the earth.

"Think of what the surface was like a million years ago. How might it be like a million years from now?"

Who was asking her that, and why had she never thought about that before? She wanted to ask Romey and Sam if they realized what they were walking on, but when she started to speak, they told her to shush, be quiet, listen to Bovert.

It was easy to do. Molly liked Bovert. He was a kind and gentle teacher. He seemed to know everything about plants and animals. Because of him, everything in the forest began to be familiar, known, simple.

"Be a cougar," he told them. "Like this!" And Bovert was suddenly a cougar, padding quietly in circles around them, purring, being a cat.

"Be an eagle," he told them. "Like this!" And Bovert was an eagle, circling over them, screeching, being an eagle.

"Be a fish," Sam laughed in Molly's face. "Like this!" And Sam sucked in his cheeks, widen his eyes, and moved his lips open and shut.

She tried to be a bird. She wanted to be a bird. She wanted to fly like Romey had flown with the bird feathers. But when she tried to fly, to be a bird, she felt a pain in her arms and head . . . .

"Don't try so hard, dear. Relax. Cool down. Try to eat . . . ."

Who was talking? Was that Bovert?

"Don't try so hard. Just be," Bovert smiled.

Then he pointed out what to eat, what not to eat, what to touch, what not to touch among the many plants in the wild. With Bovert, the woods and fields held tranquillity and made sense in its arrangement of all living creatures. Why don't I just stay here? Plenty to eat. But I'm not hungry now.

Time! What time is it? Doesn't matter. There's no such thing as time. It's all made up. It feels good being formless, airy, part of what Sam and Romey were doing. Yet, she didn't really feel part of it either. She watched as they learned the patterns of the animals, to be the animals.

"Look," Bovert told them. "Observe and understand grazing animals, like antelope, deer, and bison. Watch so you can become smaller creatures, such as snakes, rabbits, moles, chipmunks and squirrels."

He moved them to water's edge where they watched beaver, mink, and otters. In the air they identified all types of birds from sparrows to eagles.

I'm Molly the sponge. I'm absorbing. I ... I'm wearing the story.

"A new lesson!" Bovert announced. He made them watch as a snake easily swallowed whole an unsuspecting mouse as it come out of its hole. Molly felt sorry for the mouse and wondered how Romey felt. Later, a hawk—or was it a falcon—seemed to dive down from nowhere, grabbed the snake and disappeared into the air.

I don't like this lesson.

Then Bovert took them into the forest where squirrels were roaming in hoards of acorns they had collected. They seemed playful and appeared to be having fun. Molly watched Romey and Sam laugh as they observed the animals stand on their hind legs and examine acorns in their front paws. They seemed to be separating acorns into two piles.

A jaguar leaped unseen on one of the animals, caught it with sharp claws and dragged it away in its teeth. Only a little gray-brown fur, bloodied, lay next to some acorns.

Whoosh! They were standing in a large field of tall grass where several antelope were grazing. Molly wasn't sure if she was really there anymore. Maybe she was watching Bovert, Romey and Sam on some huge television or movie screen. Yet, she felt she was there. Yes, the air felt hot and humid, and she had trouble breathing in the heat. Surely, she must be there, too.

"It's too hot," Molly heard herself say.

In panic, the antelope sprang into movement, hooves pounding.

Did I scare it?

No, it was the cheetah leaping up out of the high grass and pouncing on one of the smaller animals running behind the herd. Romey didn't like what she saw either, Molly could tell. Sam just made a face and muttered, "Whoosits."

Not pretty sights, a sadness came over them.

"This is part of nature," Bovert explained. "You're seeing part of nature's food chain at work."

"But those poor little creatures," Molly replied.

"It's nature's way of supplying continued food energy from one living thing to another. Each creature consumes a lower member and in turn is preyed upon by a higher member. Life is cyclical. What dies eventually helps something else live. Except for humans, animals kill only to eat."

What's wrong with hmans, Molly wondered.

Bovert's voice began to fade. Then Bovert himself. Now Sam and Romey started fading from Molly's view. She called out, "Don't go. Stay. Please stay. I don't want to be alone."

But soon Molly could no longer see them or hear them, and she found herself standing all alone, surrounded by tall trees. She had no idea where she was or what to do.

Her skin felt hot and sticky, her vision blurred. She tried to speak but her mouth was too dry. Even breathing hurt. She fell to the ground, saw herself lying there on the forest floor. She watched as her fingers dug into the soft mossy earth. Why wasn't she feeling the earth between her fingers? Was it possible to be outside herself? Was that her there, lying prone and still now? Had she left her body? Where had Romey—Sam—Bovert —gone?

A dark shadow moved toward her and began to inch over her body. Molly watched it move slowly over her feet. It felt cold. Then it inched over her legs, up toward her stomach. The heat she had felt slowly began to give way to the cold of the dark shadow.

"No, not yet."

Whose voice said that?

The shadow stopped moving. Faintly, like a voice bouncing in a cave, she thought she heard, "It's not her time."

The shadow disappeared. Her body seemed to rise. Her eyes cleared for a moment and she thought —yes— she was looking into Romey's face.

"Romey? Is that you?"

Romey was—what— carrying her? Yes, she was sure of it. There's the gold medallion with the oval ruby in one of the settings.

Then her eyes grew too tired and heavy and they closed. But the image before her of the ruby and the me-dallion twirled—twirled—twirled. She reached out to touch it ...

When Molly opened her eyes again she saw the faces of her mother and father floating in front of her. Their con-cerned faces wouldn't stay still and kept floating, twirling in front of her. Romey's face joined those of her parents.

"Romey," Molly whispered. "Thank you." Romey gave a fragile smile.

"What, dear? What did you say?" Her mother leaned closer to Molly's lips.

"Romey?"

"It's mommy, dear. Daddy's here, too."

"Romey. She saved me—from the—from the cold shadow." Molly's eyes closed again and her face held on to a slight smile.

Molly heard her mother ask her father, "What did she say about Romey?"

"That Romey saved her from a cold shadow."

"Romey? What does she mean? Saved from what? A cold shadow?"

Molly opened her eyes and saw the baffled look on her parents' faces, then smiled and closed her eyes again. She heard her parents talking.

"I don't know what she means. She's delirious."

Molly felt her mother's hand on her forehead.

"Her fever's broken. She feels much cooler. I think the worst is finally over."

"Strange." It was her father's voice.

"What?"

"Oh, just that she's so wrapped up in the Romey stories. I didn't realize they were so much on her mind."

Molly felt her forehead being wiped with a cool cloth and a light kiss on her cheek. Her mother.

"Hmm. Yes, well, Molly's always had a vivid imagination."

"That's for sure." There was a pause. "Wha ..."

"What is it? What's the matter?"

Hearing her mother's worried voice, Molly wanted to open her eyes, but couldn't.

"Look at this. Look what's in Molly's hand. And the other one."

"Now where did this come from?"

Her parents' words faded as Molly slipped into a peaceful sleep.

Clutched in Molly's hands was fresh smelling mossy dirt.

CHAPTER 6

Two days later, Molly was feeling better but not well enough to get out of bed. She felt weak and often dozed off. When her parents asked her about Romey, the cold shadow, and the dirt in her hands, she tried to explain what she remembered. Her parents excused most of what Molly told them as part of her illness, but her explanation of how the mossy earth got in her hands still remained a mystery.

On the afternoon of the third day of Molly's illness, Molly's mother had gone to her clinic and her father sat in Molly's room reading by her window while she slept. The curtains, pulled open wide, let the sunlight filter through the maple tree into the cheerful room.

"Dad?"

"Right here, kiddo. How you doing?"

"OK, I guess.

"Good. Can I get you anything?"

"No, thanks." Molly looked out her window and remembered the day she and her mother had planted her tree. She had been too young to really be of much help, but she felt so proud when they finished. The tree had grown so quickly. Bovert would know all about her tree. There must be trees like hers in Rairarubia.

"Dad?" Her voice sounded raspy and weak.

"Hmm?" He looked up from his book.

"Tell me another Romey story."

"Now?"

"Please. I don't feel like sleeping or reading. It's boring lying here."

"Romey, eh? I guess you are getting better. "

"You don't believe me—I mean about Romey saving my life, do you?"

"Well, I wouldn't say that exactly. I think you believe that happened, but ..."

"Doesn't the dirt you found in my hands prove anything?"

"Well, let's say it certainly does make things more difficult to understand." He went over and sat on the edge of her bed.

"It's true, though. I was grabbing at the ground, the shadow was ..." Molly tried to sit up.

"OK, OK, don't get excited. If you believe it, I believe it." Her father gently pushed her back down and brushed some hair from her eyes.

"Please, then? Just a short Romey story?"

"Well, you'll have to tell me where we left off. I've forgotten."

Molly retold what she remembered about the class verte as best she could. She could tell her father became quite confused when she told him about the snake, the hawk and the cougar, and Bovert's explanation of the food chain. She continued to add the part about Romey saving her life.

"Well, let's change the story a little and go back to Bovert's lessons, OK?"

Molly knew that because she was sick, her father didn't want to challenge her too much on her story. "OK," she agreed in a weak voice.

"Well, as you can imagine, Bovert turned out to be a very good teacher. During their time with him, Sam and Romey learned about everything one could know about nature and surviving in it. Several months went by. Once Bovert was sure they had learned all he could teach them, he decided it was time for them to be tested.

"You've both done well," Bovert said. "It's time for

your test."

"I was hoping you'd forget about that," Romey replied.

Bovert smiled. "Not likely. It's why you are here."

"So what's the *test*," Sam tensed at the word, "like?"

"You will both be sent out on your own."

"Alone? Whoosits!"

"Sam! Will you *please* quit saying 'Whoosits'!"

"What?"

"Whoosits! Whoosits! You're always saying 'Whoosits'!"

"I am? Well, really, I ..."

"Excuse me, you two, but we must be getting on with the test," Bovert interrupted. "Our right timing is everything."

"Timing? What do you mean by 'our'?" Romey felt sure this was just one more mystery she would not have answered but had to ask Bovert anyway.

"All in good time."

"That's what I thought you'd say," Romey muttered.

Bovert continued, "You will both be sent out alone to live in nature on your own. The test is to see how well you can survive by using what you have learned from your time with me."

"But why?" Romey asked, and then added before Bovert could answer, "I know, I know—all in good time."

Bovert nodded, and Romey noticed a slight smile he tried to hold back. But Bovert's smile quickly vanished as he held out a six-inch long knife in each hand. The blades were three inches wide, encased in leather sheaths, with pearled handles.

"Other than what you have learned, these knives are the only thing you can take with you." Bovert continued to hold out the knives. Sam picked one and drew it from its sheath, admiring it.

"Whoos ... sorry," Sam said, catching himself. "This is some knife."

At first Romey didn't want to take the other knife from Bovert, but then reluctantly accepted it. "I guess it could come in handy."

She didn't draw the knife from the sheath, but slipped it under her green sash. Sam continued to examine his knife as Bovert began explaining the class verte test.

"Now I must blindfold you both. When you hear my voice, you may remove the blindfold. Do not remove it until you are told, otherwise it could be very dangerous. When you remove the blindfold, you will be on your own."

"How long will we be on our own?" Romey asked as Bovert placed a thick black cloth over her eyes and tied it behind her head.

"Until it is time," Bovert answered and then, after waiting for Sam to put away his knife, blindfolded Sam in the same way.

"Well, Romey, see you around," Sam joked nervously.

"Good luck, Sam."

Romey could see nothing and hated not knowing what she was getting into. But, she told herself she'd survived all the mystery stuff so far, why not one more.

"Remember, Romey and Sam, what you have learned. You are about to enter nature. Be nature. Expect the unexpected and all will go well."

With Bovert's last words, Romey felt a wind on her face grow stronger and stronger, almost pushing her over. The noise of the wind became louder. The ground waved under her. Again came the cold, then the hot air. Soon the wind and the noise stopped. Romey started to take off her blindfold, but then remembered that Bovert had said to wait for his voice.

Romey grew impatient standing there, wherever "there" was. Finally, she heard Bovert's voice in the distance telling her she could remove the black cloth.

It took her eyes a few moments to adjust to the daylight again, but when they did, she found herself in the middle of a quiet forest. Sam and Bovert were nowhere in sight. Although she was in an unfamiliar place, Romey recognized many of the trees and plants Bovert had taught her to identify. That made her feel somewhat more comfortable, but not much. What if she couldn't take care of herself? What if she forgot important things Bovert had taught her, like what to eat, what not to touch? Did she really understand what he meant by "be nature"? What if she couldn't pass the test, whatever it was?

"Well, I guess I'd better think more positive and start proving I learned how to survive," she told herself half aloud. "Keep alert and keep your wits. Expect the unexpected. Keep alert and keep your wits."

Judging from the position of the sun, Romey believed it was mid-morning. That would give her time to look for a good place to make camp. It should be near water, she decided.

After searching for what seemed an hour, Romey came upon a shallow, running stream about six feet wide. She followed it until she found a large, flat grassy area that looked like a good spot to make her camp. "Well, old girl, what kind of camp shall it be?" she asked herself.

Around the edge of the grassy area, Romey noticed some saplings and fallen trees. That reminded her of the small lean-to that Bovert had shown Sam and her how to make from them. After examining the fallen trees and branches, Romey began hauling out the ones that looked best for the frame. It wasn't easy dragging them by herself.

"Sam, I never thought I'd miss you and your 'whoosits', but I sure wouldn't mind your help or your company right now," she admitted aloud.

Romey went to work breaking off and cutting five frame poles with her knife. She used the knife to dig deep holes for each of the two standing poles and buried them deep for support. She tied the other frame poles together with strong, thin, green branch shoots that she could bend easily. Then cutting smaller branches to size, she tied them one against the other until she had fashioned the sloped roof and the sides. To fill in the cracks between the roof poles, she mixed water, dirt, and dried leaves together, then spread the mixture over the poles to dry.

"There." Romey stood back and looked at her work. It was large enough for her to sleep in and to store fire wood. "I think Bovert would be pleased with it."

Moving along the edge of the clearing, Romey gathered several arms full of firewood and stacked it all neatly inside her lean-to. Then she went to the water's edge and began looking for the flint stones Bovert had taught her to use to start a fire.

By the time Romey finished, it was late in the afternoon. Her hard work had made her very hungry.

"Now comes the really hard part." She paused a moment, then said to a tree. "Well, would you look at me? I'm talking to myself. Well, why not? Nobody can hear me, and I doubt if you understand me, anyway." She patted the tree on the trunk. "Or do you? Wouldn't surprise me around here."

Romey began searching for something to eat, remembering what Bovert had taught her to avoid. Near her campsite, she found some bushes thick with blackberries. Being hungry, she forgot how thorny the bushes were and scratched her hands and arms in her hurry to pick some. She slowed down after a few mouthfuls and decided she had better find something else or she would get sick from eating just berries.

As Romey stood deciding which direction to take, she felt something moving across her left foot. She looked down to see a long, thick rattlesnake weaving a path between her legs.

Her first flushed reaction was to kick it away, but something in her thought, no, "Be the snake. Be the snake. Be the snake." As she said the words over and over, she felt herself relaxing. Her eyes closed, yet they still seemed to follow the gray and black designs on the body as it slowly glided over her foot.

"I am the snake." She felt the rough dirt underneath her pearl white belly as she slithered in search of food. "I am the snake." Her tongue darted in and out, sensing her surroundings, eyes of little use. Her body had no feel of bones, only hunger. Thoughts only of searching, searching, searching.

Romey opened her eyes and looked down. The snake was gone.

The snake's hunger had mixed with hers. She understood the snake's need. With a different frame of mind, she continued her search for her own food.

Romey soon discovered an apple tree, but the lower apples she could easily reach were all pecked open by birds. The ripe, shiny red ones were all too high up. So Romey climbed into the tree to get to the ripest ones.

Once in the tree, she sat there for a while eating. Then she picked two more and put them inside her green sash for later. She also made a mental note to remember where the tree was.

"Well, now, that's a good start. But I'm still hungry."

The light was beginning to dim, so Romey decided she'd better stick close to her lean-to area. She made a circle back toward her camp and noticed wild asparagus half hidden in the weeds. She picked as many of the long slender stalks as she could before it was almost too dark to tell what she was picking.

On her way back to the lean-to, Romey was feeling good about what she had accomplished when . . .

"GRAAACK!"

Romey froze. She'd never heard such an ugly, frightening noise. Then she heard it again.

"GRAAACK!"

It sounded as if it were coming from near her lean-to. Very slowly, walking silently as Bovert had taught her,

Romey made her way toward her camp. What in the world was it? The sound was like nothing she had heard in her training. Bovert said to "be nature," but she wasn't sure she could be whatever was making that sound.

"GRAAACK!"

It grew louder. She was getting closer. She pulled her knife from its sheath and crouched low in the brush. Her heart pumped in double time. She spread some branches so she could see. There, by her lean-to, Romey saw it.

Molly's eyes closed, then popped open when she realized her father had stopped.

"Don't stop," Molly murmured trying to keep her eyes from closing. "I'm not asleep."

"I think that's enough for now, kiddo. You rest, and I promise we'll get back to Rairarubia tomorrow. OK?"

"OK." Molly knew she was about to fall asleep again.

"Good girl. I know you're not feeling too well when you don't protest for more."

By the time her father kissed her goodnight and turned off the light, Molly was asleep.

CHAPTER 7

"So, how's the patient today?" Molly's mother sat on the side of the bed and felt Molly's forehead.

"OK, I guess. I just woke up." Molly yawned and sat up a little bit. She still felt weak, but at least she'd had a night with no dreams.

"Well, I want you to stay in bed today. Doctor's orders. It's going to take a few days for you to get your energy back."

"I'm missing a lot of school."

"You'll catch up. Don't worry about it now. Just rest and take your medicine."

"Ooo, mom, it's disgusting. It tastes awful. " Molly made a face.

"Maybe, but it's helping you get well, so just be a good girl and brave it. Want some breakfast?"

"No, not yet, thanks."

"Well, I have to get to the clinic." Her mother kissed her on the cheek and stood up. "I'll try to get home early tonight. Yell for your dad if you need anything."

After her mother left, Molly lay in bed looking out her window. Things felt so different in the daylight than they do at night. She thought about the black shadow and Romey saving her. Had she just been dreaming? Everything had seemed too real.

"Hey, kiddo, how's it going'?" Her father broke her thoughts and came into her room with some cranberry juice and a muffin. "Brought you some breakfast." He placed them beside her bed and sat next to her.

"Thanks, but I'm not very hungry."

"You need to eat. I promised doctor mom I'd get you to eat something."

Molly had an idea. "How about this. I'll eat if you go on with Rairarubia."

"Oh, now it's blackmail, is it?" he smiled.

"Yep."

"I don't know. You're not supposed to give in to blackmailers. They just may come back for more."

"And I just might," Molly said.

"Tell you what," he said, "I'll continue the story if you eat."

"Now you want to blackmail me."

"Let's call it a compromise."

"OK, but you have to tell it while I eat."

"Deal," he said and offered his hand. Molly took it and they shook.

"Well, let's see. Where were we?" Mr. Doogan took off his shoes and sat next to Molly on her bed. He leaned against the headboard.

"You know, kiddo, I'm not sure where this story is going myself. The whole Rairarubia thing had taken on a life of its own."

Molly started to say, "More than you know," but decided it was better to just get on with the story.

"There was a bad noise—a grack-like sound at her lean-to camp, remember? Romey was sneaking up on it." Molly leaned against her father and put her arm through his.

"Right. Well, guess what?"

"What?"

"I really don't know what made the noise."

"You don't?"

"Nope. Any ideas? I need your help here."

Molly thought for a minute. "I think it should be something weird. Maybe like an animal Bovert didn't teach her anything about. You know, maybe he wanted to see how she could handle unusual situations."

"Hmm. That might work. Let me think now."

"Yikes and spikes!" Romey said to herself when she saw the creature. It was nothing like any of the animals Bovert had taught her to live with. Its white head was round like a ball. It had only one eye, deep red, and two nostrils about the size of a quarter. She couldn't see any ears or mouth. Its blue-green body looked like a horse's, but the front legs were smaller than the back legs, like a kangaroo's. And its tail was curled, almost like a pig's, but stuck straight out. It looked so silly she didn't know whether to laugh at it or fear it.

Romey watched as the creature stuck its head into her lean-to. She noticed its neck could stretch out from its body like Silly Putty as it moved in and out and around her newly made camp. It sniffed around like a dog picking up a scent.

Suddenly, it raised its head and let out another "GRAAACK" that was so loud it hurt Romey's ears. The head turned in her direction and stretched out toward where she crouched even lower. The head bobbed up and down, its one red eye blinking slowly as if it had trouble focusing in the fading sunlight. After a moment, it turned and slowly moved on its hind legs across the stream and disappeared into the grove of trees on the other side.

Romey stayed low for a while longer, wanting to make sure the creature wasn't coming back. Then she cautiously crept back to her lean-to. It now had an terrible odor that Romey decided must have been left by the creature.

"Phew! Stinko!" Romey said to herself. "And I've got no choice but to sleep here tonight."

The sun had gone down and the twilight made everything around her campsite seem pink. The stillness felt a little eerie. Romey quietly made her way down to the stream for a drink. Then, worn out from the day's events, she crawled into her lean-to, keeping her knife next to her in case the strange creature decided to return. A wave of loneliness washed over Romey. But before long, the wave receded and she fell into a tired sleep.

The next morning, Romey awakened with the sunlight shining on her face. Her loneliness had disappeared with a good night's sleep. She reminded herself why she was there and that at some point it would be over. Getting up, she felt stiff from sleeping on the hard ground. "Gotta' do something about that before tonight," she told herself.

Then she noticed that the scratches on her arms from berry picking were swollen and looked infected. Just looking made them itch. Romey immediately searched out some plants that Bovert said had healing power. She found an aloe plant, broke open one of the pods and rubbed the liquid inside on the scratches. The itching and healing began almost instantly.

"Hey, thanks, Professor Bovert."

That day and the next, Romey spent most of her time gathering food and exploring her surroundings. She kept an eye out for the weird creature, but there was no sign of it. In addition to gathering berries, apples, and wild asparagus, she found some edible roots and bird's eggs, being careful not to take all the eggs from one nest. She also gathered some dead leaves and fashioned a softer bed under her lean-to.

On the third day, Romey started getting bored and occasionally lonely. How long was she supposed to live in nature alone? What was the point of this? Hadn't she proved she could live alone? What else was she supposed to be doing here? When was Bovert going to come for her?

With nothing else to do, Romey decided to walk up the stream to see if she could find its source. The stream ran fairly straight with only a few turns here and there. The farther she walked, the wider the stream. In a few places, pools were deep enough for swimming.

Just as Romey was about to turn back, she heard what sounded like a waterfall. Continuing on, she rounded a bend and there it was. Water dropped from a four-foot knoll into a small pool that fed the stream. Climbing the edge to the top of the fall, Romey looked out on a sapphire-colored lake several miles around. In the middle stood a small, palm-tree covered island.

"Would you look at that!" Romey said aloud. She felt like Columbus.

Her first thought was to get to that island. But how? It looked too far to swim. She remembered how her last swimming adventure had turned out.

Romey walked along the edge of the lake, looking for anything that might help her get to the island. Finally, she saw a rather large log washed up along the lake bank. It occurred to Romey that she could hang her arms over the log and kick her way over to the island. When she had to rest, the log would keep her afloat.

She slipped off her boots and dragged the log into the water. Surprisingly, the water was warm. Once Romey could no longer touch bottom, she draped her arms over the log and began kicking her way toward the island. She watched the island grow larger as she moved along more quickly than she thought possible. It wasn't long before she touched bottom and walked ashore, dragging the log up with her.

Unlike the terrain she just came from, the island seemed another land. Tall palm trees swayed slightly from a hot breeze that musically fanned their broad accordion-like fronds. Shorter trees stretched their thick, leafy branches out like umbrellas. On the ground, large ferns and colorful tropical plants sprouted here and there among the trees and tall bamboo shoots. The air was already drying her wet clothes.

Romey began to explore the island. It contained things not available back across the lake. She found pineapples, papaya, mangoes, bananas, and coconuts. Sugar cane stalks grew clumped in large patches.

"This is a regular market place."

It occurred to Romey that she could build her camp here where there seemed to be more food, but the heat felt too uncomfortable.

"I need to get some of this food back to my place. But how?"

As she scratched her head thinking of an answer, Romey spied some long, broken bamboo shoots lying on the ground.

"Of course! That's it, " she told herself. She began to gather up as many of the longer stalks as she could find, placing each one next to the other on the ground. Soon she had gathered or cut enough shoots so that she had a three-foot wide stretch of bamboo. She then cut some vines growing around the trees and used them to lash the bamboo pieces together. When finished, Romey stood back and looked at her raft.

"There. That should do it."

The heat was beginning to get unbearable, the air almost too hot to breathe. Romey dragged the raft down near the log she'd left at the water's edge.

As quickly as she could, she gathered a variety of the food the island contained. She even found some gourds she could use to hold water. With her raft filled, she pulled it into the lake, draped her arms over the edge and pushed the raft in front of her.

It took a little longer to get back to shore where Romey had left her boots. Once there, she had the task of carrying her cache back to her lean-to. And her camp was at least a mile back along the stream. By cutting another piece of strong vine and tying it to the raft, Romey managed to pull the raft down the stream.

Occasionally, the water ran so rapidly that she had to get in the water and guide the raft around rocks or debris. In other places, she had to pull the raft over shallows. Twice she almost lost everything. But eventually, she made it to her lean-to.

She just managed to store her new found food before dusk. Her clothes were still wet and the evening air felt chilly. Using the flint stones she had found, Romey started a fire. She smiled in puzzlement at how hot the island was compared with her camp site. But the fire felt good, and she felt tired from the day's work. The scratches on her arms were almost gone.

Later, when the fire had turned to embers, Romey curled up on her new bed of leaves. She was just drifting off to sleep when ...

"GRAAACK!"

The ringing telephone brought the story to a halt.

"Oh, no, don't answer it," Molly said.

"I have to, kiddo. I'm expecting the call. Business." As her father left her room, he called after him, "Finish your muffin. That was the deal."

It seemed to Molly that the story was always getting interrupted at a bad time. But she finished the muffin and drank the juice as promised.

The day dragged by for Molly. Her father came in once in a while, but he was on the phone or at his computer most of the time. She tried to read but her head and eyes still hurt a little. She got up long enough to have lunch with her dad, but was ordered back to bed afterwards. She wished she were well enough to go back to school. Being sick was no fun. She couldn't even have any friends over.

But the day passed and soon Molly's mother stuck her head in the bedroom door.

"So, how's the patient?"

"Hi, mom. I'm sooo bored. This has been the most boring day."

She came in and sat on the edge of the bed. "Ah, a sure sign that you're getting better."

"The only good thing that happened today was dad telling me a little more of Rairarubia. We got interrupted by a phone call. Then he had to work."

"Well, how is your Romey these days?" Molly's mother felt her forehead again and then examined her neck and throat.

"The weird creature has come back to Romey's camp."

"Well, it's obvious you're feeling better. Good. Now, then," her mother said, scooting closer to Molly on the bed, "tell me about this weird creature."

After Molly filled her mother in on the story, her mother asked, "You know, honey, we still can't figure out how you got all that dirt in your hands the night you were so sick. Now that you're feeling better, can you tell us?"

"You mean the night Romey saved me from the dark shadow?"

"Well, it's a little difficult for you to understand. You were hallucinating feverishly. You thought that's what happened."

"But it must have happened. That's how I got the dirt in my hands. I was grabbing at the earth, trying to get up when the shadow came and Romey saved me. Honest, mom. That's all I remember. Why don't you believe me?"

"Well, dear, I'm sure it all seems real to you. I guess it's my scientific mind. I just need a better explanation. Here, put this thermometer under your tongue and close tight but don't bite."

Molly opened up and felt the cold silver tip under her tongue.

Her mother looked at her watch. "But all this talk about Rairarubia does make me wonder if these Romey stories are good for you."

Molly pulled the thermometer from her mouth. "Mom! Come on. Dad wouldn't tell me a story that's not good for me."

"Not on purpose, anyway. Now, put that thing back in your mouth. I want to make sure your fever is gone."

Molly did as she was told. They were both quiet

until her mother took the thermometer and checked it.

"Good. Back to normal." Molly tried to smile back at her mother's.

"Maybe dad will tell some more tonight, and you can listen in. Okay?"

"We'll see how you feel after dinner."

That didn't sound too promising to Molly.

CHAPTER 8

That evening, Molly felt well enough to call Netty.

"So, when you comin' back to school?" She could hear Netty chomping and popping her gum.

"Dunno. When my mom says it's okay. Am I missing much?"

"Nothin' you can't get caught up on. Oh, and Blake got sent to the principal's office—again. Threw a book at Pauly." More chomping, popping.

Molly had other things on her mind besides Blake's bad behavior. She wanted to tell Netty about her feverish dream, if it was a dream. But Netty wasn't very understanding the last time she told her about Rairarubia. But she just had to tell someone.

"Listen, Netty, some really weirdo things have been happening to me."

Molly told Netty everything about the dream where she thought she was in Rairarubia, about the shadow of death, about Romey saving her life, about the mossy dirt under her fingernails that no one could explain, how she knew her mother didn't want her dad to continue with the story they'd made up.

"I know she thinks the story is having a bad effect on me," Molly said.

"Well, it is. Listen to you. You make it sound like there *is* such a place as Rare-a-whatever and all and that Romey's a real person." Chomp, chomp, pop.

Molly sighed. "I know. I'm not sure what to think

any more. But it's like—well—like I'm involved somehow. Oh, it's too hard to explain."

After talking with Netty, she felt well enough to eat dinner with her parents. She could see the relief on their faces now that she was recovering. Still, she felt a little weak afterwards and was willing to get back in bed. Besides, Molly thought the chances were good that her father would return them to Rairarubia.

Sure enough, not too long after dinner, Molly found herself sitting in her bed with a parent on each side. It was a safe, comfortable feeling. Plus, she was happy that her mother wanted to hear more about the weird creature.

Mr. Doogan began, "Well, remember, Romey was just falling off to sleep when she heard ...

"GRAAACK!"

The strange creature sounded very close. Romey grabbed her knife and crept into the bushes to hide. No sooner was she hidden when the animal appeared. Enough of the fire was left for her to see. It slowly stepped toward Romey's lean-to, stood up on its hind legs, and then stretched its long neck into the lean-to. Swinging its small head back and forth, it began knocking down one side of the lean-to.

Seeing her hard work being wrecked, Romey sprang from the bushes, waving her knife in the air. "Hey! Leave my place alone! Get away from there, you —you silly snodderclout!!" She was too angry to be afraid and forgot all about trying to "be the creature."

The strange animal drew its head out from the lean-to and stretched its neck toward her. "GRAAACK!"

"Don't you 'graack' me, you silly looking—stupid—smelly old—poopnoddy!" Romey couldn't think of any other words. She stood there, flustered, knife in hand, not really knowing what she was going to do now.

The creature's round head bobbed around, seeming

not to be able to focus its one red eye. Then suddenly it rolled over on its back, legs in the air, like a playful dog wanting its belly scratched.

Romey wasn't sure what the beast was doing. She carefully took a step toward the thing, then another, then another.

The creature just lay there, its head swaying slowly back and forth like a metronome set in slow time.

She thought about Bovert. "Now, how am I supposed to be you?" Slowly, Romey reached out, quickly touched the animal, then withdrew her hand.

"Mooawk."

Was that a sigh? Did the thing like being touched?

Romey dared to touch it again. Its skin had the texture of a pig. Bovert had missed the boat on teaching her about this animal.

"What are you, anyway? I'm not sure I'd want to be you. You're silly looking and you stink."

"Mooawk," it sighed again.

Growing more bold, Romey rubbed the belly of the creature while it occasionally murmured mooawks.

"Well, you sure made a mess of my lean-to." Then it occurred to Romey that the creature might have been looking for the food she had stored in her place. She got one of the bananas she brought back from the island and held it out near the creature's head.

She still didn't see any mouth. But before she knew it, the banana was gone from her hand. The creature's mouth just opened from somewhere in its head, then disappeared in a flash.

"Ah, so that's it. You're hungry."

She held out another banana, which disappeared into the hidden mouth as quickly as the other one.

"Some mouth you've got," Romey told it as she rubbed its belly some more.

"Well, I guess I'm going to have to forgive you for wrecking my home. To think I was angry at you. Well, you're still a big clodhopper."

Romey continued rubbing and patting the animal while it mooawked softly.

"Well, are there more like you? And what shall I call you?"

"Mooawk," the creature sighed again.

"Yeah, mooawk to you, too," Romey laughed. "Hey, that's it! I'll call you Mooawk."

Romey fed Mooawk a papaya, then decided that was enough. She was tired and needed sleep. Even though her lean-to was partly wrecked, she could still sleep in it for the night. She'd fix it tomorrow.

"Okay, Mooawk. Bedtime. Roll over or something. I'm going to bed." Romey bunched up her bed of leaves into something halfway comfortable and stretched out. Something about having Mooawk there made her feel less lonely.

Mooawk didn't move. It just lay on its back and rested with its neck on the ground. For some reason, Romey lost any fear of Mooawk and soon fell into a sound sleep.

When Romey awoke the next morning, Mooawk was gone. Romey actually felt a little sad. At least Mooawk was some company, and she didn't like the occasional lonely feelings that swept over her.

Romey spent most of the day repairing her lean-to and gathering more food. She wove a small container for storing food and filled the gourds from the island with water from the stream. She gathered enough firewood for the next few nights. Several times during the day, she hoped that she would see Mooawk again.

Chores done, Romey explored downstream for a few hours. She found a nice pool for bathing and splashed around for a while. Then she stretched out on a flat rock to dry in the sun and closed her eyes.

Not long after, Romey felt a shadow over her face about the same time she smelled something foul. She opened her eyes to find Mooawk peering at her.

"Whoosits!" Romey sat up quickly, ducking under Mooawk's long neck. "Don't *do* that!"

Mooawk raised its neck out of the way and then rolled over on its back. Its one eye seemed to beg Romey to scratch its stomach.

"Well, I have to say I did miss you a little today." Romey gently rubbed and scratched Mooawk's belly. "You disappeared on me."

"Mooawk. Mooawk."

"Yeah, you like this, huh. You're like a big old dog."

Then the peacefulness was shattered.

"GRAAACK!"

The bellow was nearby and louder than Mooawk's graacks. Mooawk jumped up and raised its neck high as if to listen.

"Not another one!"

"GRAAAACK!" This one sounded bigger.

With that, Mooawk took off in the direction of the bellowing, leaving Romey alone again.

She waited for a moment but there was no more bellowing. Sunset wasn't far away so Romey made her way back to her camp site. Why hadn't Bovert told her about creatures like Mooawk, she wondered. And did she really say "Whoosits" back there? She admitted she missed Sam. And what was she doing here, anyway? Maybe she should have left that cave way back when she had the chance.

But she hadn't. So here she was. *She* had made the choice. It was all her own doing. "I've no one to blame but myself, girl," she told the flint stones as she struck up a fire and settled for the night.

The next several days went on into weeks and were often boring. Romey quit thinking about time. She continued to collect food, water, and fire wood. She explored more new territory and made several trips to the island. During that time, she never saw Mooawk.

Then one day, she wasn't sure how much time had

passed, Romey discovered a cave entrance that was mostly hidden by brush. With her knife, she cut and tore away at it until she could make her way in. As her eyes adjusted to the dark, she saw it was a very large and deep cave. Realizing she would need some light, she searched around the mouth of the cave for some sticks she could use as torches. Luckily, she found some flint near by, struck a fire, lit one of the sticks, and entered the cave.

Not far in, the passageway split, both heading downward. For no particular reason, Romey decided to start exploring the left side. As she went deeper into the cave, the ceiling grew higher and the air cooler. The only sound was the flickering of the flames of the torch.

The deeper she went, the colder it got. But Romey kept on. After burning two of her torch sticks, she finally came to a wide, deep chasm. When she looked over the edge, she couldn't see the bottom even with her torch. If she wanted to go on, she would have to jump at least four feet across.

"No thanks. Turn around time," she said, hearing her voice echo against the cave walls. She started back the way she came when …

"GRA-AA-CK!"

The creature's echoed cry hurt her ears. The sound bounced around inside her head like a wild ping-pong ball. But then there was another one, closer.

"GRAAACK!"

The ground shook under her feet. A stale, disgusting smell invaded her nose, and then there it was.

A much larger version of Mooawk lumbered toward her. It was hard to tell the difference between it and the torch light shadow cast along the cave wall. The creature's head appeared to be stretching out toward her, wanting to get there faster than its body could carry it. This one's mouth was visible and it kept snapping open and shut. Its one eye flashed a fiery blood red in the torch light.

"GRAAACK!"

It didn't take Romey long to realize she wouldn't be scratching that creature's belly. She also realized she could not get past the thing coming toward her. That meant she had to jump the bottomless chasm behind her or be snapped up in the jaws of the creature. At the moment, jumping sounded better.

Quickly, Romey returned to the edge of the chasm. She knew she needed a running start if she were to make it across. So she turned back toward the thing coming at her, turned again when she saw that red eye almost on her, and ran as fast as she could to the edge and leaped.

"Molly, look." Her father nudged her gently and nodded his head toward his wife. Molly smiled when she saw her mother's head leaning back against the headboard, eyes closed, mouth slightly open.

"I guess Rairarubia's not too exciting tonight," her father whispered.

"Well, it is for me. Don't stop now," Molly whispered back.

"I think we'd better stop. You need your rest and so does your mom. She's been working pretty long hours this flu season." As he got up from the bed, his wife awoke.

"Oh, my, I guess I dozed off. Sorry. What did I miss? Is Romey still in the cave?"

"We've decided to leave things hanging in the air for tonight." Mr. Doogan winked at Molly.

"Oh, real cute, dad."

CHAPTER 9

The next night after dinner and a game of *Clue*, Molly's parents thought she should get to bed early. But Molly, after some pleading, convinced her parents they should not keep Romey suspended in the air any longer.

Recovering nicely, Molly still felt a bit weak, but she insisted she couldn't get to sleep unless she heard more about Romey. So they all made themselves comfortable in Molly's bed again.

Molly filled her mother in on the part of the story she had missed the night before, which turned out not to be much.

"Well, I agree, Molly. Your father never should have left poor Romey hanging like that."

"Yeah, the meany."

"Hey, Romey's tough. She can take it," her father said in self-defense.

"Well, come on, then, let's get on with it," her mother prompted.

It seemed a leap into forever. Then Romey felt a sharp pain from her ankle to her knee. She lost her balance, fell face down, and began sliding backwards on her stomach toward the deep opening below. Her fingers clawed and scraped at anything that would hold, but she kept sliding and began to drop over the ledge.

Just as she thought it was all over, her green sash caught on a jagged rock and she stopped sliding.

Her dangling, searching feet found a small toe hold. Using all her might, Romey managed to reach one elbow up over the ledge. Struggling with all her strength, she stretched the other elbow over. With that leverage, she wiggled and pulled her way up over the edge and crawled safely up to the flatter edge of the chasm.

"GRAAACK!"

Romey held her ears. She had forgotten about the creature during her ordeal. Now, breathing in relief, she sat looking over the chasm at the swaying head, its red eye flashing in anger. Try as it might, it couldn't stretch its neck across to her side.

"Oh, go graack yourself," Romey yelled across, rubbing her sore ankle.

"GRAAACK!"

She held her ears again, then yelled back, "Stupid snollgoster. You almost got me killed."

With one last "GRAAACK" the creature turned and disappeared back into the depths of the cave leaving Romey's ears ringing.

She sat for a bit rubbing her ankle and leg. Her body ached and now started stinging from all the cuts and scratches.

When the flame in the torch she had dropped started flickering, Romey looked around for the other torch sticks, but could only find one. She lit it from the dying one and decided she'd better find a way out of the cave soon. No way could she ever get back across that chasm from this side.

For what seemed forever, Romey limped her way along the small ledge. Her torch was burning down. She started to worry that she just might never find a way out. What had she gotten herself into? Was all this part of the test? Did Bovert or anybody know about this cave? Between her aching body and her fear that she might never get out of the cave, Romey wondered if she'd failed the test and this was her end. Would she die never knowing who she was?

Then she felt a rush of warmer air. As she moved along, it kept getting warmer. She hoped that meant something good.

A few minutes more and she saw it. Light filtering in. A way out! She ran ahead, ignoring her pains.

Ducking her head slightly, Romey passed through the opening with a sense of relief. The hot air and the brightness of the sun kept her squinting for a moment, but it felt welcomed after the dark cave. As she became used to the light again, she looked around and realized where she was.

She stood at the top of the small island she had been swimming to with her raft. The cave was another way to reach the island. But only if she wanted to deal with the possibility of running into the creature.

Romey went down to the water to clean up her cuts and scrapes. On her way, she picked some fruit and filled her empty stomach. She also rubbed some special plant leaves Bovert had shown her on her cuts and bruises. As she walked around the edge of the island, she found the log she had used to help her float kick to the island the first time. She pulled it into the lake with her and slowly kicked her way to the shore. After her cave experience, the water felt good on her sore body.

Dark by the time Romey made her way to what she now called "home," she built a fire for the night and slept until the sun was fairly high in the morning.

Romey, stiff and sore the next morning, didn't feel much like exploring. Using palm leaves she had brought back from one of her trips to the island, she spent most of the day weaving a floor mat for her lean-to and a hat for herself. After lunch, she decided to go down to one of the pools in the stream for a little splash.

On her way she heard it again.

"GRAAACK!"

"Oh, no! Tell me I'm hearing things."

"GRAAACK!"

It was coming closer.

"No, I'm definitely not hearing things."

Spotting a tree with low limbs, Romey climbed up as far as she could. Looking toward the sound from which the creature's cries came, Romey gulped.

She saw *three* of the funny-looking creatures! One of them was humungus! Maybe the one from the cave. Another one was slightly smaller, but not by much. Then there was the little one. Could it be? Yes, Romey realized, the small one was Mooawk.

The two adult creatures seemed to be fighting each other. They stood on their back legs and swung their long necks at each other as if they were trying to knock the other off balance. The smaller creature tried to hide behind what Romey assumed was the mother.

Fearsome and sad to watch, their fighting brought them right under Romey's hiding place. The creatures smashed their necks and heads against the other so hard the ground shook. They butted heads and yelled out ear-shattering graacks. But it wasn't long before the larger creature got the best of the mother. One swift, hard swing of the big one's neck finally knocked her off balance. It tore at the mother creature's throat and reminded Romey of the scenes Bovert had shown them about the food chain.

But this time it didn't seem right. It didn't appear that the big creature was killing to eat. Romey knew she was right when the big creature suddenly turned on Mooawk. One swing of the big one's neck and Mooawk was on the ground next to its fallen mother. Just as it was about to rip into Mooawk's throat, Romey screamed, "NO!"

She jumped from the tree, knife in hand, landing on the neck of the killer creature. It swung its neck swiftly back and forth like a dog shaking off water, but Romey held on with her arms wrapped around its neck. It tossed its head up and down, back and forth. Still, Romey held on. But the shaking was so fierce that she had no chance to use her knife or she'd be tossed off. And all the shaking and twirling about made Romey want to throw up.

While all this was going on, the mother creature recovered her senses and could see her attacker was in trouble. Somehow, gathering her strength, she managed to rise up. With a long, well-aimed, powerful sweep of her head, she caught the big creature off guard, knocking it off its feet.

It fell hard, trapping Romey under the long, heavy neck. She tried to crawl out from under, but couldn't move. The big creature struggled a moment, then fell still. The wounded creature had somehow finished off her attacker.

"GRAAACK!" The wounded mother let out a sad cry.

Romey struggled to get out from under the heavy neck, but couldn't move. Then she saw Mooawk's head over her.

"Mooawk."

The mother's larger head, its red eye dim and droopy from being wounded and weary, gently pushed Mooawk aside and stared down at Romey.

"I hope you're too tired to be hungry."

Then the mother's head moved away and only Mooawk stood there nodding its head, making little mooawk sounds.

Romey, worried what the mother creature had in store for her, began to feel movement in the heavy body she was trapped under. At first, she thought maybe the big creature was still alive! She felt around for her knife, but couldn't find it.

Then she realized the mother creature was pushing the dead one away from Romey. With a little squirming, Romey soon pushed herself free. But before she could get up, the mother's head appeared over Romey again, stared down at her, then opened its hidden mouth. Its breath made Romey choke. Instead of biting Romey, it dropped something from its mouth, almost hitting Romey in the head.

"GRAAACK!"

Somehow, that cry didn't sound as sinister as other

ones had. And with that and a soft "Mooawk," the two creatures moved off into the trees.

Romey looked down at the object the creature had dropped from its mouth. It was the dead one's red eye.

"Yikes and spikes!" She moved away from the slimy red thing.

But as disgusting as it looked, Romey couldn't take her eyes from it. Then something strange began to happen. The eye began to move like a Mexican jumping bean. Then its shape changed. It shrank a little, rolled, seemed to turn harder and shinier as she watched. It kept shrinking and changing shape. Then the movement stopped.

Romey rubbed her eyes to make sure she wasn't seeing things.

The ugly red eye had turned into a sparkling, diamond-shaped ruby.

Romey smiled and picked it up. She felt sure she knew what it meant. She reached inside her shirt and pulled out the medallion. As she snapped the ruby into the empty diamond-shaped setting, a heavy, white cloud enclosed Romey. Within it, she thought she heard a dim voice say, "Well done, Romey. You have shown courage and intelligent use of your training. You have proven you can expect the unexpected. You have passed the test."

Then came the changing feel of temperature on her skin, a soft wind sound. She felt herself being lifted, and she knew she was being transported somewhere. But where? What was next?

"That makes two rubies she's earned," Molly said with a big yawn.

"And two to go, right?" her mother asked with a yawn.

"Right. Seems she's heading for another class and another test," Mr. Doogan answered, getting up from Molly's bed, stretching and yawning himself. "Now, you get some sleep, kiddo." He gave Molly a kiss and left.

"I hope I don't dream about those creatures." Molly was sorry she said that, knowing how her mother felt about the effect of the story on her.

"Just call on Romey, if you do," her mother smiled as she turned out the light. "She seems a pretty capable young girl."

Her mother's comment made Molly feel better. "So," Molly said, "you don't think the story's bad for me?"

She bent down and kissed Molly's cheek. "I just worry about your taking the story too seriously, that's all. Now, good night and sweet dreams."

"I hope so," Molly sighed. "I really hope so."

CHAPTER 10

Molly lay in the dark having trouble falling asleep. She did not want the graacky creatures in her dreams. Then she remembered when her teacher had told the class as a joke not to think about an elephant. But all she could think about *was* an elephant. So as she drifted off to sleep, she decided to think about Romey. Romey seemed so real to her. She'd like to be like Romey, have the courage of Romey.

"Romey, Romey, Romey," she started saying half aloud. She tried picturing Romey jumping fences, like when you count sheep. But she only got to forty-four. Then she pictured Romey and Sam together, recounting their adventures in her head. Then she wondered what it would be like if Romey were her older sister.

Ah, yes, Romey, I wish you were my sister. You could teach me so much. We'd have so many great experiences together. I'd even share this room. Oh, my! Just listen to me! You're not even real.

Molly scooted lower in bed and turned on her side. She felt sleepy.

Romey, she thought, sometimes I see you so clearly—in that funny cloud—being carried off somewhere—having exciting adventures—the voice telling you well done—what will your next test be—would Romey see Sam again?

"Romey, Romey, Romey. What would it be like to be you? Romey . . . Romey . . . where is the cloud taking you now . . . Romey ?"

The cloud kept Romey from seeing anything. She felt some movement, but couldn't really describe it—like floating, but not exactly that either.

Then Romey felt her feet on sandy ground. The cloud and noise slowly disappeared and she found herself in the middle of a circular arena. Up above the arena walls were several rows of stone seats, all empty. She turned around, gasped, and jumped back, automatically reaching for her knife. In front of her stood the largest man she had ever seen.

He said nothing, just stood there, stern looking, his bare muscled arms folded across his huge chest. He wore a white sleeveless shirt and white pants tucked in black boots. A wide, black sash was wrapped around his waist. Curly, fire-truck-red hair tied into two long braids trailed down his back. He wore a headband with the letter **R** set inside a triangle.

Romey, hand on her knife handle, stared at the giant's green eyes that looked her up and down. Despite his size, which was fearsome, Romey did not feel totally afraid, just a little. Neither moved and no words were spoken for several moments. She was determined not to be the first to speak. Probably, she felt, this mountain of a man was part of another trust test she had to undergo. At least, she hoped so.

Finally, the giant spoke.

"So little one, welcome, " he bellowed. "I like you. You show no fear. Good. I am Herman. I will be your teacher for a while." His even teeth were big and a bright white against his dark skin.

"Teacher of what?" Romey replied, trying not to let her voice quiver with the anxiety she was really feeling.

"I am the teacher of the class forte," Herman replied with a serious tone and narrowed eyes. "It's my job to make you strong and quick, and to teach you the art of fighting—and winning."

"Fighting? I don't like fighting. What if I don't want

to fight? Who do I have to fight?"

"Ah, you may not want to fight, but you will have to. If you are the chosen one, that is."

"Oh, boy, here we go again. What do you mean 'the chosen one'?"

"The designated one. The one we have been waiting for. So far, you have passed two of the tests. If you pass my class ..." Herman's voice trailed off.

"I keep hearing that. But nobody ever explains anything to me." Romey's irritation flared up. "Who or what is this designated one, anyway? Why me? Why was I selected? And now you want me to learn how to fight? I don't want to fight anybody. Fighting is stupid. I'm not mad at anybody."

She stood with her hands on her hips looking up at the huge man.

"As you say, little one, fighting is stupid. But sometimes one must fight to protect those who would do harm to others for no reason but self gain or power. And if one must fight, it is best to know how to protect oneself and others from those who do want to fight, who may even enjoy fighting. As to the rest of your concerns, all in due time." Herman's voice grew gentle and calm.

"All in due time. That's all I ever get."

"No, it is not. Think, Romey. Think what you know now that you didn't know before you found the medallion you wear."

Romey touched the medallion and ran her fingers over the two rubies. In her mind, she remembered the bird who swept her away, finding the medallion, then the cave, the choice she was given, Sam, the castle of Rairarubia, the mean one they call Mammoth, Bovert, learning about nature, the chain of life, surviving alone, saving Mooawk.

"But I still don't know who I really am or where I come from."

Herman merely stood there, saying nothing.

"Yeah, I know—all in good time," Romey sighed,

resigned. "Well, let's get on with it, then. But I still don't like the idea of fighting anyone."

"That's an appropriate attitude," Herman replied. "First, we must build your body to endure great physical strength. Let me see you run. Run around the arena a few times."

"Run?" Romey made a face.

"Yes, run, as fast as you can."

Running was not one of Romey's favorite things to do. Mumbling to herself, she started trotting around the arena.

"You call that running?" Herman yelled at her. "That's not running. That'll never do! Lift those legs higher. Stretch those strides!"

And that began Romey's first day of training, training that was to last many months.

Immediately, Romey was put on a daily exercise program to build up her strength. Herman controlled what she ate, when she could rest, when she could sleep. When she wasn't being trained, which was almost always, she slept in a small room under the arena stands. The room held only a bed, a table and a chair. Her breakfast and dinner meals always appeared mysteriously on the table. She never saw anyone bring the food or take away what she left, which wasn't much once her training became more rigorous. Herman always had snacks and drinks he gave her during the day.

And Herman worked her hard. In the beginning her body ached from muscles she didn't know she had. Sometimes she wished she were back at her lean-to, doing as she pleased. At really bad moments, she even wondered if the giant bird's nest would be better.

But over time, she learned to run faster, pacing herself for miles. She lifted various weighted bags of sand to strengthen her arms and legs.

She trained in gymnastics. She even learned how to do a standing front or back somersault over Herman's head, something she didn't believe was possible. She learned how to walk on her hands for ten to fifteen minutes at a time. She easily did perfect cartwheels all around the arena without stopping. She became expert at high jumping, pole vaulting, and javelin tossing.

At times, she felt Herman was too hard on her, yelling at her when she made stupid mistakes. But inwardly she began to enjoy the training. Her body become stronger and she liked the feeling. When she mastered a skill, she felt good about herself. And she was getting very, very good.

Then one day after she had run around the arena for five miles, Herman handed her a smooth, seven-foot long stick, almost her height.

"What's this for?"

"Hit him with it," Herman told her.

"Hit who?"

"Him. Hit him with it. As hard as you can."

From nowhere, a figure suddenly appeared next to Herman. It looked to be a normal-sized person, dressed like Herman except for the hood that covered its face.

"Who's he? Where'd he come from?" Romey puzzled, trying to see a face inside the hood.

"Hit him! Hard!" Herman's voice said impatiently.

By this time Romey had learned that Herman meant what he said. So, she held the stick firmly and swung at the hooded figure.

Before Romey could blink, the stick was in the faceless stranger's hands.

"How'd you do that?" Romey said, truly amazed. She had felt nothing leave her hands. She again tried to see the face under the hood.

"Hit it again, and watch more closely," Herman ordered.

Romey took the stick back and tried hitting the unknown person again, but once again the stick disappeared without feeling from her hands. She still didn't see how it was done.

It took Romey two weeks before she learned how to hit the hooded figure without having it take the stick from her. But once she learned the combination of concentration and swiftness she began to catch on.

Then one day during practice, after she had mastered the technique, she struck the hooded person with the stick and it disappeared. It just vanished.

"Wha … where'd it go?" Romey looked about, but there was no one but Herman and herself. She still held the stick.

"You're ready for kendo," Herman said. He didn't seem a bit surprised that the figure had disappeared. And by this time, Romey was too used to the unexpected to be surprised by much.

Kendo, Romey soon learned, is the ancient Japanese art of fencing with bamboo sticks. Along with kendo, she learned karate and kung fu. Again her partners were always mysterious hooded, faceless figures who seemed to evaporate whenever Romey became proficient in the skills being taught.

Even though months of training went by, Romey continued to be unaware of the passing time. She was kept too busy. At night, she fell asleep quickly, tired from the day's training. Occasionally, during meals or brief rest periods, Romey questioned why she was going through all this training, felt lonely, and surprised herself at how much she missed Sam. Romey often wondered what had happened to him and promised herself if she ever saw him again, she'd never complain about his "Whoosits." But whenever she asked about him, the answer was always "in due time." At least that gave her hope that she might see him again when her training was over.

During all this training, Romey's body grew taller and stronger as she mastered one skill after another.

Once her physical strength allowed it, Herman taught her how to use a long bow and the crossbow. After a few lessons, she could send off ten arrows within thirty seconds and hit the center of the target with each one.

She also learned to fence with thin foils as well as broad blade swords. Training in the use of a shield and a chain mace came next.

One day, Romey showed up for training as usual and found Herman holding the reins of two horses. The jet black one had a white, arrowhead-shaped spot between its eyes. The other was opposite—all white with a black, arrowhead-shaped spot between its eyes.

"Take your pick." Herman made it sound more like an order than a request. Romey had yet to see him smile during her training, even when she did things perfectly.

"The black one."

Herman handed the reins to Romey. The horse was big and had no saddle.

"I've never ridden a horse before," Romey told Herman as she patted the horse's shiny black neck.

"You'll soon learn. Mount up."

Romey started to ask how she was going to do that, the animal being so tall. But then she remembered her gymnastic training. She stepped back from the horse a few feet, then took two running steps and leaped on the horse.

But the horse seemed startled and reared up on its hind legs. Romey tried to hang on to its long mane, but felt herself slowly slipping . . . slipping . . . slipping down the horse's black back.

"Ooohh! Nooo!"

She hit the ground hard. Looking up, she saw four jittery hooves about to trample her.

"NO!" Molly yelled.

Her own yelling woke her up. For a moment she didn't know where or even who she was. Then it slowly dawned on her. She was on the floor beside her bed, covers on top of her.

"Romey?"

Molly rubbed and blinked her eyes as she looked around her dark room. All was quiet. The only movement came from her curtains, silently billowing from a slight breeze coming through the window, shadows of the maple tree dancing against the wall and ceiling.

CHAPTER 11

Molly, still half asleep, got back into bed, pulling the covers from the floor back over her. Partly, she felt glad Romey's fall had been only a dream, but part of her wanted to be back in Rairarubia. She lay on her back, staring at the leafy shadows on the ceiling made from the moonlight, so different in the daylight.

Why couldn't she be like Romey? Maybe even *be* Romey. Wouldn't it be great to have such adventures, to be so brave? And now that Romey was getting stronger, bigger, and learning how to do so many things—fun things—exciting things.

"My life is so boring in comparison," Molly muttered, settling back into bed.

Molly yawned and her sleepy eyes mindlessly continued to watch the silent shadows swirl about over her head. At first, the images held no shape, but as Molly continued to gaze she thought she saw something.

A figure? What's that? Horses—no, one horse—a big, black horse—up on its back legs—front legs pawing at the air—then down—stomping the ground. Who's on the ground? Romey?

The fast moving horses' hooves seemed all over the place. But thanks to the training Romey had, she rolled quickly out from under the nervous stamping feet. Unharmed except for the loss of some pride, she stood back from the black horse, wondering what to do next. She

looked at Herman, still holding the reins of the white stal-
lion.

"Talk to the horse, Romey. Tell it that you mean it
no harm, that you want to be one with it. Let it know that
you are aware of its power, that you want to use that power
for good."

Herman motioned toward the black horse. It stood
still now, its head nodding as if to agree with Herman.

Romey approached the horse and pulled its head
down to hers. She stroked between its eyes and began
whispering in its ear.

"Easy, now, big boy. Let's be friends. I never rode a
horse before, okay? So give me a break. I don't want to
hurt you. And I don't want you to hurt me. I don't even
know what all this training is about, but I guess you're part
of it. So let's work together. Let's be one, like Bovert and
Herman say. You be me and I'll be you."

Romey patted the smooth, shiny black hair of the
horse's neck. She could feel the strength and power in the
muscles under the long mane.

"Now, let's try that again."

Ready in case she was thrown once more, Romey
leaped on the horse's back. This time, the horse stood its
ground.

"Good boy." Romey reached down and pulled up
the reins.

"What now?" Romey asked Herman.

"Close your eyes. Feel the power. Be one."

Romey shut her eyes. She was no longer just sitting
on a horse. She and the horse were one. Her legs were the
horse's, strong, agile. She was power, speed, endurance.

"Open your eyes," Herman directed.

When she did, Romey realized how high from the
ground she was. Herman, the huge, looked smaller. Her
range of vision was farther, wider. She understood what
Herman meant by being one with the horse. She understood even more now what Bovert meant by being one with

nature.

During that moment, Romey felt she needed no lessons on riding. As if by magic, she knew what to do. After a few turns around the arena, she and the horse dashed through the gate and sped across the open field outside. Like one being, they raced at the speed of a flying arrow. They jumped hedges and gullies so high and wide, they seemed to soar in the air for minutes at a time. When they returned, Romey felt she had been part horse all her life.

"Enough for today," Herman ordered.

Romey hated to quit, but knew it was useless to argue with Herman. She dismounted, patting the black flanks of the horse. By comparison, she felt small again.

"What's his name?"

"That's up to you," Herman said matter-of-factly.

"Well, then, I think I've got a great name for you," she told the horse. "You're black as night and fast as an arrow. Black Arrow."

The horse raised its head up and down as if agreeing.

"Come, now. Your last lesson awaits."

"Last lesson?"

"Yes. You are almost ready."

"Ready for what?"

But as Herman said the words, Romey sighed and echoed them knowingly. "All—in—due—time."

"Put these on," Herman ordered, handing her a pair of soft leather moccasins.

Romey knew better than to ask Herman why, so she pulled off her boots and put on the moccasins. They were light tan, plain except for the letter R on the bottom of each one, and fit perfectly.

Herman led her to the open arena door and pointed to the flat field beyond.

"Now run."

"What?" Romey was used to her boots and the moccasins, as soft as they felt, did not seem fit for running.

"Run, Romey!" Herman ordered.

"Okay, but I'm not going to be able to run as fast as usual." Romey broke into a run, but to her surprise she seemed to move better and faster than ever. The moccasins made her feet feel light, almost like she was wearing wings. Then she really cut loose, running so fast that everything she passed was a blur. At one point, she realized she was running along side a startled deer.

No, not along side. She passed the deer!

"These are fantastic!" she told Herman upon returning. "They're magic moccasins."

"Yes, Romey. They are magical. But the magic can wear out. You must only use them when necessary, not for fun. You have grown very strong during your time here. You can run fast on your own. The power in these moccasins must never be abused. Do you understand?"

"I think so." Romey couldn't take her eyes from the moccasins.

"No! You can't just think so. You must *know* so. Do you understand?" Herman was always serious, but this time his voice almost pleaded for her to say she understood completely.

"Yes. I understand. I must only use them on very special times. They are not for fun."

"The magic can wear out," Herman warned her.

"How long will the magic last?"

"It depends on the circumstances," was all Herman would say. Then he handed her a pair of gloves. They looked to be made of the same material as the moccasins.

"Put these on."

They fit Romey perfectly. As she was admiring them, Herman handed her a bow and quiver full of black-tipped arrows.

"Shoot an arrow in the air."

As she had been taught, Romey pulled an arrow from the quiver, locked it in the bow string, pulled back, and let the arrow fly. With a slight singing, the arrow disappeared out of the arena.

"Yikes and spikes!" In all her training, Romey had never shot an arrow that far or with such force.

"Now, shoot another arrow out of the arena, then run and catch it before it lands."

Romey looked at Herman as if he were crazy.

"You can do it," he told her assuredly.

"You want me to shoot an arrow and go catch it before it hits the ground? Impossible!"

"You can do it, Romey." Herman sounded impatient.

Not so sure herself, Romey pulled another black-tipped arrow from her quiver, shot it in a high arc, then ran, keeping an eye on the flight of the arrow. To her surprise, she kept pace with the arrow and was there to catch it as it descended.

"I don't believe this!" She stood there holding the arrow in one hand. "I did it!" She ran back to Herman with the arrow.

"Magic gloves, too?" She kept looking at her hands and her feet.

"Like the moccasins, Romey, the magic power of the gloves is limited. You must only use them when your normal skills will fail you. You do understand, don't you?"

"Yes." Romey was still stunned by all the magic powers when Herman handed her a small leather pouch pulled closed by a leather thong that was woven in and out of the opening. She looked up at Herman with questioning eyes.

"This pouch contains the biggest magic of all. Open it."

Romey pulled the small pouch open and looked inside.

"Sand?" Romey didn't understand.

"Not sand, no. It is a magic powder ground by the ancients from very special stones."

"A magic powder?"

"Yes. But there is just enough powder for three uses."

"To use for what?"

"If you find yourself in grave danger, sprinkle a small amount of the powder in a circle around you. Nothing will harm you if you stay inside that circle."

"What kind of harm do you mean?" Romey didn't like hearing this.

"Any harm of any kind to your life."

"Are you telling me I may be in harm's way soon?"

"I'm merely telling you that this powder has strong magic and that you must use it with caution. Remember, there is only enough for three uses."

"The way you say 'only three uses' doesn't sound like a happy thought. How often am I going to be in danger of my life, anyway? And what has all this preparation been for? You and Bovert—and Sam. What's happened to Sam?"

Romey felt frustration again at the lack of answers to her questions, never knowing what all these tests were for.

"I'm tired of 'in due time'. It's time for some answers," Romey demanded.

"Yes, it is time for some answers." Herman looked at Romey and smiled for the first time since she had started her training. Then he waved his arm high and brought it down quickly.

Before she could blink, Romey found herself standing in the middle of the arena. She was no longer wearing the moccasins or the gloves, but was back in her boots and regular clothes. Her quiver full of arrows was on her back, her bow draped over one shoulder. Strapped on a belt around her waist was a sword and a knife.

Taken by surprise, she looked down at herself and yelled, "Herman, what's going on here?"

Then a doorway in the wall of the arena slid open and out stepped another figure, dressed and armed just as she was. At first it just stood there. Then it began to move toward her, drawing its sword.

Romey immediately drew her sword, not certain what she was supposed to do. Was this a test? Was she ready? Was she to fight this figure? If so, why? Who was it? Was this the Mammoth coming at her? Was this what all the training was about?

As she stood her ground, the figure came closer, sword raised and then suddenly rushed toward her!

"Molly, honey, wake up." Somewhere deep in Rairarubia, Molly heard Romey's voice.

"Be careful, Romey."

"Molly. Wake up, honey, you're dreaming."

Molly opened her eyes to see her mother smiling down at her.

"You're dreaming, honey. I heard you tossing and moaning. It sounded like you were having a bad dream. You've fallen out of bed."

"Oh, mom. Romey has to fight somebody." Molly's words were covered with sleep.

"Ah, not Romey again." Her mother pushed Molly's hair back from her face, helping her get back in bed.

"It was so real. Before now, I woke up and the curtains — the shadows on the ceiling—the horse. It's like—I became Romey."

Her mother smiled. "It's all fine dear. You're still recovering from a very bad case of the flu. Medicines can sometimes cause you to have vivid dreams."

"But with Romey, it never feels like a dream. It's so real."

"I think your imagination—and your father's—are getting the best of you two. Well, anyway, do you feel well enough to come down for some pancakes? Want to sleep more?"

"No. Breakfast sounds good. Be down in a minute."

Molly, aware of something in her hand, instinctively knew she didn't want her mother to see it. But once her mother left the room, she opened her hand.

It was a small, black arrowhead.

CHAPTER 12

During breakfast, Molly didn't mention the arrowhead, even though she wanted to. Her parents were already puzzled by the dirt they had found in her hand during her feverish state. Now the arrowhead. She couldn't explain it, but felt that if she showed it to them, they would get upset, maybe stop the stories.

They did ask her about her dream, so between bites of pancakes soaked in syrup she filled them in.

"Hey," her father laughed, "maybe your mother's right. That Romey girl we created is getting bigger than the both of us." Then he quickly added, "Any more pancakes?"

"There's more batter in the bowl. Put one on the griddle for me, too." Then Molly's mother added, "Really, now, I'm beginning to wonder whether we should continue these stories. They seem to be giving Molly nightmares."

"They're not nightmares," Molly spoke up quickly. "They're just, you know, dreams. And I like them."

"From what you just told us, they're getting more violent. What was that you said—kendo fighting? And bows and arrows, maces, sword fights. I don't know." Her mother shook her head and gave a false shudder. "Not the stuff I thought about when I was a girl. Why can't you have Romey involved in more pleasant things."

"Geez, mom, come on." Molly was positive now that she wasn't going to show the arrowhead to either parent.

"This is all your fault, you know." Her mother pointed her empty fork at her husband.

"*Moi? Petit moi?*" Her father made an innocent face. "Anyway, what's wrong with a good, old-fashioned sword fight?" Molly smiled as her father waved the pancake spatula around like a sword. "You know, like King Arthur, the Green Knight, Robin Hood, the great Duke of Dooganville."

Molly laughed. Her mother smiled, but added, "I don't like violence. Don't burn the pancakes while you're dueling."

"But, mom. Romey doesn't like fighting either. She has to learn to fight because she has a mission, right dad?" Molly wanted her father to be on her side.

"A mission? Have we gotten to a mission yet?" Her dad wasn't being the help she wanted at the moment.

"You know. What about the Mammoth? Isn't she going to have to fight the Mammoth? He's the bad one, making everybody miserable in Rairarubia."

"Mmm, right. The Mammoth. I forgot. You're getting a bit ahead of me."

"Well, you said this was our story. You wanted my help, remember?"

"True enough. But I think your mother wants us to tone things down." Waving the spatula in the air, he comically placed a pancake on his wife's plate.

"And you don't?"

"No, my lovely-scientific-minded-doctor wife, I do not. I think people don't use their imaginations enough. Too much staring at television and computer screens does little for the imagination."

"Okay, okay. Maybe I'm wrong. I just don't like to see Molly getting sick or too serious about these Rairarubia tales." She switched her attention to the pancake on her plate.

"Sick? Look at this daughter of ours." He went over to Molly and gently lifted her chin in a pose. "Does this face look sick?"

They all three laughed. But Molly couldn't stop thinking about the arrowhead she had hidden in the back of one of her dresser drawers.

That night, Molly's mother wanted the family to read together, something they hadn't done for too long, she felt.

"I want to know what's going to happen next in *A Wrinkle in Time*. It seems ages since we read it."

"Hmm, me, too. I'm forgetting the whole story," her father added.

"But Romey's about to have a fight with somebody. We can't stop there," Molly protested.

"Well, since you and your father are in charge of this story, I don't see why you can't *not* have a fight just as well."

But eventually Molly's mother lost out to her daughter's pleading, knowing Molly would never concentrate on any other story at this point anyway.

So Molly reminded her parents where her dream had ended, and her father started from there . . . .

As the figure approached, Romey pulled her sword from its sheath. She had a moment of jitters at the thought of fighting a real person, not one of those disappearing hooded training figures. But then all of her mental and physical powers merged and she readied for the fight.

The figure came charging at her and their swords clanged as they hit. Both fighters stepped back to make another charge when Romey looked at the face of her opponent and lowered her sword.

"Sam?"

"Who ... Romey?"

He lowered his sword and as they looked at each other, they broke into smiles and then laughter.

"Whoosits! It's really you. I hardly recognized you. You've grown. You're bigger."

"So have you."

They just looked at each other for a moment without speaking, both happy to be together again.

"I wasn't sure I'd ever see you again," Sam said.

"Same here." Romey smiled broadly. "I hate to admit it, Sam, but I missed you."

"I admit to the same."

After just smiling at each other and feeling a little silly, they realized where they were and what they were supposed to be doing.

"Why do they want me to fight you?" Romey asked.

"I don't know. Herman just …"

"Herman?" Romey interrupted.

"Yeah, my trainer. He told me I had to fight someone in order to move on to the next stage."

"What stage? What do they mean?"

"I don't know. Every time I ask a question, I'm told 'in due time'."

"Yeah, me, too. And I'm sick of it."

Just then another door in the arena wall opened. Romey and Sam turned and waited. But not for long. Soon six large men, all looking like the Mammoth Romey had seen at the Rairarubia Castle marched out into the arena. They lined up in a row and drew their swords.

"You both are finished!" six voices yelled in unison.

"Oh, oh," Romey said.

"Whoosits! They are big, aren't they?"

"I hope Herman taught you well," Romey told Sam as the warriors charged them with swords drawn. "I'll take the three on the left."

As if they were of one mind, both Romey and Sam pulled arrows from their quivers and each felled one of the fighters at either end of the row. But there was no time for more use of the bow. They braced for the approaching raised swords.

Herman's lessons served them both well. Romey and Sam, back to back, each brought another warrior to the ground with their swords. They now faced one warrior each.

Romey's third assailant suddenly threw down his sword and twirled a mace with a small barbed ball on the end of a chain. He lashed out at Romey's sword, knocking it from her hand with a clang. As he charged at Romey with the mace, she did a standing jump and leaped over his head, landing behind him.

Before the warrior knew where she'd gone, she flew feet first at him, landing in the small of his back, pushing him face first into the ground. Romey used her strength and training to bring both his arms around behind him. She quickly removed her sash and tied his hands together. As she pulled the sash with all her might, a small leather bag fell from his hand.

Looking up to see how Sam was doing, she was not disappointed. He had his warrior tied up, too.

"Whoosits! Nice work, Romey. Who taught you how to fight?"

"Herman the huge. Same as you, it appears." Romey bent down and picked up the small pouch.

"What's that?" Sam inquired, looking over her shoulder.

Romey opened the pouch and found a glittering red ruby in the shape of a …

"Let me say!" Molly wanted to decide on the shape for the medallion. "A square!"

"You got it, girl," her father smiled.

"That makes three. Only one to go now."

"Well," Molly's mother said, getting up from the bed, "I hope Romey doesn't have many more fights. Personally, I can't wait to get back to Charles Wallace.

"I think we can wrap up this story in the next couple of nights, don't you, Molly?" Her father bent over to kiss her good night.

"I hope so." After a pause, she added, "But in some

ways I don't want the story to end."

"Heaven forbid." Her mother smiled and kissed Molly on the forehead.

"Come on, mom!"

"Just kidding, just kidding. Sweet dreams. No more nightmares."

"That would be nice," Molly said to herself.

CHAPTER 13

After her parents left her room for the night, Molly slipped out of bed and tip-toed over to her dresser. Reaching in the drawer, she felt around until she found the hidden arrowhead. Then she crept back into bed and pulled up the covers.

In the pale light coming through her window, she couldn't see the arrowhead very clearly. At least, not at first. But the more she examined it, turning it over and over, the whiter and brighter it seemed to grow.

"How did I get this," Molly whispered to herself. "Oh, Romey, did you really bring it to me?" Then she thought how silly that was. Romey wasn't real. She was imaginary. She and her dad had made her up. Everything that happened, except her dreams, were made up.

But how did she get this arrowhead? Explain that one. And the dirt in her hands the night she was real sick. Something mysterious was going on, and she needed to know what it was. She wanted to tell her parents, but she was afraid they would stop the story telling. Some part of her needed that story, needed Romey.

She lay in bed pondering all this when she heard someone whisper her name.

"Molly."

At first she thought it was her mother, because the voice was soft. But when she heard her name again, she knew it was neither of her parents.

"Molly."

Molly's heart beat harder against her chest. Who could be in her room? She sat up, and almost afraid to, turned on her bed lamp. No one was there. She started to call her parents.

"Don't be afraid, Molly. It's me, Romey."

"Romey? Where are you?" Molly looked around her room again but saw no one. She felt blood rush to her face. Was someone playing a trick on her?

"Look at the arrowhead."

Molly looked.

"What? What about it?"

"Stare into the arrowhead."

Molly looked at the arrowhead, now bright white instead of black.

"I—I don't see anything."

"Look harder."

Molly looked again. Then, gradually, a picture began to form on the surface of the arrowhead.

"Romey!" Molly gasped. She blinked and looked away, shaken. Is this a dream?

"Keep looking, Molly. Keep looking into the arrowhead. Don't be afraid. Nothing can harm you. Come share my adventures with me. Come if you wish."

Molly felt movement, a white mist enveloped her, a dampness on her skin—like in the story.

Then . . .

"Who's this?" Sam asked.

"Molly, this is Sam. But, of course, who would know that better than you," Romey said by way of introduction.

Molly, speechless and open mouthed, could not believe she was now in Rairarubia. But here she was, standing next to Sam and Romey in the middle of the arena where the fight had taken place. The three of them.

"Who's Molly? Where did she come from? What's she doing here?" Sam didn't like not knowing what was going on any more than Romey did.

"Let's just say that she's very important to both of us." Romey winked at Molly. "If it weren't for her, we wouldn't be here."

"Well, whoosits, I'm not too sure I *want* to be here after that little fracas. And what has she got to do with it? And tell her to close her mouth. She looks silly standing there like that."

Molly quickly closed her mouth. This couldn't be happening, she thought.

But it was.

"You'll have to excuse Sam, Molly. He has yet to have any training on manners." Romey turned to Sam. "Now stop and think a minute. This is Molly. You know, *Molly* and her *father*."

Sam frowned, thinking, then. "OH! *That* Molly! Of course. Look, I'm sorry, Molly, but things have been happening so fast around here. We just had a big fight with six huge . . . whoosits, what am I telling you this for? You know all this. Silly of me, just got excited. Say, why'd you have us do that? What's going to happen next? Give us a clue."

Molly gaped at both Romey and Sam, both looking at her expectantly.

"Yes, tell us, Molly." Romey said. "All we get around here is 'in due time'."

"I—I can't."

Sam and Romey, surprised, stared at each other. Then Sam asked, "What do you mean you can't?"

"I can't because I—I don't know."

"Don't know? You have to know. This is all your doing. Don't tell me this is the end after all we've been through. A fight with people we don't know and don't even know why?" Sam threw up his arms and walked in a circle, then stuck his face at Molly expecting an answer.

"No, no. It's not the end. I mean, I—I don't think so." Molly felt flustered. This was all too real, but was it real? "I mean, yes, I want more to happen. It's just that my dad and I sort of do all this together. You know, sometimes he makes things up, mostly him, sometimes I add things, sometimes I dream things …"

"Are you dreaming now?" Sam asked.

"I—I don't know."

"You don't know!" Sam's voice went up with concern.

"No. I mean, Romey called me here. I was in my room. Was I—I mean, *am* I dreaming? Didn't you call me?" Molly turned to Romey for an answer, holding out the arrowhead.

Before Romey could answer, Sam interrupted. "Whoosits! If she doesn't know anything then who's going to tell us the purpose of everything we've done? In fact, why *are* you and I here? Is this the end of us? Oh, this is just great." Sam stomped around in another circle.

"Sam, just calm down." Romey turned to Molly and asked quietly, "Do you have the answers, Molly? Why are we here?"

Molly didn't know what to say. She didn't trust what was happening. Was she really in Rairarubia with Romey and Sam? Was she dreaming? Did Romey call to her through the arrowhead? If so, why? What was supposed to happen now?

"Look," Molly finally said, "I know my dad and I started out creating Rairarubia and you two and everything because I was bored, but something strange is happening. I mean, when I was sick with fever I thought I dreamed that Romey saved my life. Did you, Romey? My parents found dirt in my fingers the next morning, mossy dirt that couldn't have come from my bed or my room. I was too sick to have gone outside. So how did the dirt get there? And then this arrowhead!"

Molly held it out for both of them to see but went on talking excitedly. "And I thought I heard and saw Romey in it. I wanted to meet you. I wanted to share in your adventures. I live such a boring life, mostly. I wanted it to be you calling me. I guess I even wanted to *be* you, Romey. Now here I am, and I don't know how I got here."

"Oh, this is great, just great." Sam threw up his hands and sat cross legged on the ground.

"Didn't you want me here, Romey? Didn't you call me?" Molly now wished she were back in her bed at home. This wasn't fun after all. She began to wonder if she was lost in the story forever. She wanted to wake up if this was a dream.

Romey scratched her head and twisted her mouth in thought. "Look, Molly, on this side of the story, you're not even in it. I don't remember calling you. I've been too busy fighting off some pretty mean guys you and your dad sent us."

"You can say that again," Sam interjected.

Romey ignored Sam. "But, you know, maybe in some strange, unknown-to-me way I did call out to you. Maybe I wanted to meet you, but didn't know I did. After all, I don't know where I come from. Neither does Sam for that matter. Not before you and your father, anyway. But this is strange, because I know who you are. I feel a bond between us, almost like we're sisters or something. Maybe subconsciously we both wanted to meet. Maybe our minds are creating this meeting. Maybe in some way you and I are the same person."

"Oh, no! You're so brave and confident. I'd never be able to do the things you do. I could never be like you."

"Don't be so sure. There might be more of me in you than you know."

"But if I'm not in the story, how did I get the dirt in my hands, and this arrowhead?" Molly stared at the arrowhead, more puzzled than ever.

"I don't know for sure. Maybe that's my way of getting out of the story in order to understand what my purpose is."

"And mine," Sam chimed in. "Don't forget me."

"I did want to meet you." Then Molly quickly

added, "Both of you. It's so hard for me to wait for my dad to get back to your adventures. Sometimes several days go by before we get back to you. And neither my dad or I know what's going to happen. We just make it up—him mostly."

"Well, nothing's going to happen at all if you don't get back where you belong," Sam said.

"Sam may be right," Romey reflected.

"What should I do?" Molly asked.

"Go home. Back to your side of the story and let's get on with it," Sam said not too nicely.

Even though Molly was confused about where she was, she had enough of Sam's rudeness. She looked down at him now sitting on the ground and pointed a finger at him.

"Now just you listen here, Sam. If it weren't for me, you wouldn't even be here. Your purpose, whatever it is, isn't to be rude. When I get back, if I get back, I just may give you a very bad time. Maybe bigger warriors to fight." Molly surprised herself that all that came out of her mouth.

"Good for you, Molly. That's telling him." Romey clapped her hands in applause.

"What are you taking her side for?" Sam asked Romey. "She won't talk so big if she doesn't get out of here and get on with the story."

"Anyway, I just remembered," Molly added. "I *do* know something. I know that you have one more test or task. Look at your medallion, Romey. You still have one more ruby to find. Once you get that last jewel for the medallion, you'll know your purpose. I think you will, anyway."

A sudden noise caused all three to turn and see a door opening in the arena wall. Six huge figures dressed in brown karate-like uniforms and carrying kendo fighting sticks came through the opening and lined up for battle.

"Oh, oh. More trouble," Sam muttered.

"Who ordered these guys?" Romey asked.

Molly gasped. "I didn't! Honest! This shouldn't be happening. I mean, how could it be?"

"Can you fight?" Sam asked.

"No. I..." Molly felt fear rising from her toes to her hair roots.

"You have to get out of here, Molly," Romey warned.

"How? I'd love to, but how? Oh, geezohman, this can't be happening."

The six brown figures seemed even bigger as they moved toward them, their long sticks at the ready.

"Oh, geez. I don't understand this. I thought I wanted to be here, thought I wanted to be you. But I don't. I really don't. I want to go home."

"Listen, Molly, try staring into the arrowhead again. That's how you got here, maybe that's how you can get back."

Molly opened her hand and stared at the arrowhead.

"Please, please, I just want to go home," she kept repeating as she stared into the sharp, white object.

"Don't look up, Molly. Keep staring into the arrowhead. Are you ready, Sam? Here they come."

The dark figures advanced closer and started yelling and rushing toward them.

Romey's voice began to fade. "Don't look up, Molly. Look into the arrowhead."

"I just want to go home. I just want to go home."

"Molly, are you all right, honey?" Dr. Doogan peeked into Molly's bedroom.

Startled and confused, Molly didn't answer. She looked at the arrowhead and then at her mother.

"Oh, mommy, it worked! I'm home."

"Where else would you be? I heard you talking and thought you were calling for us." Her mother sat next to Molly and felt her forehead.

"You don't feel feverish. Were you sleeping? Bad

dream again?"

"Yes, I mean no, I—I—it was too real. I was really there."

"Where, dear?" Her mother smiled, but confused over Molly's state.

Molly knew her mother would never believe her. She tightly closed her hand, concealing the arrowhead. She wasn't really sure herself what she had experienced. Had it all really happened? How was it to be explained?

"I guess I was dreaming or something," Molly decided to say.

"Well, do you want me to sit with you until you fall asleep again?"

"No. Maybe. Yes, please."

Whatever had happened, Molly wasn't ready to go wherever she'd just come from. Nor was it easy for her to get the image of the kendo warriors charging Romey and Sam from her mind.

It was quite a while before Molly fell into a restless sleep, still clutching the arrowhead.

CHAPTER 14

When she awoke in the morning, Molly still held the arrowhead in her hand. Had she found this arrowhead long ago and forgotten about it? No, try as she might, Molly could not remember ever having an arrowhead before. Especially one that could change from black to white. So, where had it come from? Things just weren't making sense. Is it possible for things in dreams to appear when awake? She was totally mixed up.

Before going to breakfast, Molly again hid the arrowhead, now black again, in her dresser drawer. She didn't want to think about it anymore. Molly wanted to go back to school, back to Natty and friends.

Molly's parents agreed she was well enough to return to school. She was more than ready and felt school would take her mind off last night's dreams. If that's what they were.

But concentrating on school subjects wasn't easy. A little behind in her studies, she couldn't take part in some of the class discussions. And as hard as she tried not to let it happen, her mind frequently wandered to Romey and Sam. She had left them there just as a fight was to begin. She had been scared. Should she have stayed? Did the fight happen after she left? Would they—did they win the fight?

Now, that's a stupid thought, she told herself. They're just made-up people. She needed to remember that. She and her dad can make them do anything they want.

Or can they, she wondered?

At lunch, she just had to tell Netty what happened last night. When Molly told her how she thought she actually went to Rairarubia and met Romey and Sam, Netty broke out laughing.

"Oh, bonkers, sure you did. Come on, Molly, I think you've seen *The Wizard of Oz* too many times." She touched Molly's forehead. "Or you're still sick." Then she added, "In the head."

Molly felt tears in her eyes. She realized how unbelievable it all was. Maybe she *was* still sick. Or maybe the sickness had done something to her brain. Maybe she was going crazy. Her body shook with sobs.

"Hey, sorry. Didn't mean to make you cry," Natty said, "but you have to admit ..." She didn't finish.

"I know it all sounds too crazy. I shouldn't have told you."

"Sure you should. That's what friends are for. I shouldn't have been such a smart mouth."

"But you don't believe me, do you?"

"It's pretty hard to, Molly. I think you think it's all true. And I personally think it's all from being sick, you know, the fever, the medicine, all that stuff. I don't know what to tell you or how to help. But—like, it's all pretty far out, you know?"

"You're tell me! I'd like to think that's all it is. But what about the arrowhead? The dirt under my finger nails? Some of the story feels so—so *real* ."

"Yeah, well, maybe now that you're back in school things'll get back to normal."

Molly hoped so.

After lunch, the school day dragged on endlessly. That afternoon and evening, Molly spent catching up on her homework, interrupted occasionally with thoughts of last night's confusion. But as time slipped by, she began to think that it had to have been a dream. Her imagination had just gotten the best of her.

But then what about the object hidden in her dresser

drawer? That still couldn't be explained. And the dirt her parents found in her hands? She told herself to quit thinking about it. Just forget it.

That night, when it was story time at the Doogan's, Molly's father seemed eager to return to Rairarubia. When asked if she was ready for the story, Molly surprised herself with her answer.

"I don't know; maybe not tonight."

"What?" her surprised parents said in unison.

"Maybe we should get back to *A Wrinkle in Time*. Mom would like that."

"Hey, I know what I said, but don't stop on my account," her mother protested. "I'd like to see your story ended."

"Well," her father said, "this certainly is a first. Of course, we don't have to, but Rairarubia was on my mind for some reason today, and I came up with some good ideas about where to take the story. Maybe even end it."

The thought of ending the story gave Molly mixed feelings. Part of her didn't want the story to end, but another part of her thought that if the story ended, maybe so would her confusion. And she needed to end the distraction the story was causing or the men in white coats would be coming after her.

"Okay, then. Go ahead, dad." She saw that pleased him. He was actually enjoying making up the story. So the three of them settled down on her bed for the story.

Her dad began. "Well, now, remember that Romey and Sam had just defeated the six warriors and obtained the third ruby for Romey's medallion. Well, just when they thought they were finished fighting another door in the wall of the arena opened and ..."

"Out came six more warriors," Molly piped in.

"Yes, my thoughts exactly!" Her father began again. "This time, Romey and Sam had to engage in ..."

"Kendo."

Her father gave her a strange look. "Yes, kendo. Are

you reading my mind or something?"

"Or something," was all Molly answered. Sorry she'd said anything, she decided to keep quiet for the rest of the story. She felt sure now it hadn't been a dream. She knew what her father was going to say. Her insides started feeling funny.

Her father went on, "The six warriors, wearing brown karate-like outfits came charging and yelling at Romey and Sam who suddenly found they were no longer holding swords, but fighting sticks."

"I'll take the three on the right this time," Romey told Sam.

Before he could say anything, sticks clashed. Romey was too busy defending herself to see how well Sam was doing. But thanks to her kendo training and gymnastic ability, she soon easily felled her three warriors. When she looked around, Sam was just giving a final blow to the last standing fighter.

"Hey, we make a good team," Sam offered.

"What took you so long to finish that one off," Romey teased.

"I was just toying with him." Sam smiled and leaned on his stick.

"Well, what's next?" Romey wondered.

She didn't wonder long. Again, an opening door appeared in the arena wall. The pair stood at the ready for what ever was to come next.

To their relief, out walked Herman, leading Black Arrow and the other white horse by the reins.

"White Arrow!" Sam exclaimed, taking the reins of the white horse from Herman.

"You know that horse?" Romey was taken aback.

"Sure. I learned how to ride on him." Sam patted White Arrow affectionately on the flank.

Herman handed Black Arrow's reins to Romey.

"Good to see you again, big fella." Romey put her head against Black Arrow's neck.

At this point, Sam and Romey understood that they had both been taught separately by Herman and his mysterious hooded trainers. How, Romey couldn't figure out, since Herman trained with her all day long.

"Herman, what if Sam had wanted Black Arrow, too?" Romey was curious.

"But he didn't," Herman replied and then went on. "You both have proven ready. You are skillful warriors and athletes. You are matched in powers. But you alone, Romey, now have the magic moccasins, gloves, and powder." Herman handed all three to Romey.

"Magic what?" Sam interrupted.

Herman stopped talking and just stared down at Sam in irritation. Sam got the message.

"Sorry."

"Do not misuse the magic," Herman went on. "Their power is limited in use, remember. If you use your intelligence, you will know when and when not to use them."

"I hope you're right." Romey felt she was assuming a heavy, unknown responsibility.

"For both your sakes and Rairarubia's, so do I." Herman looked down at Romey, a bit strangely, she thought. Then he did something he had seldom done the whole time she had been in training.

He smiled, a huge smile, showing even white teeth and dimples she never expected in a man so big. He picked up both of them and gave them a big hug.

"Good luck, little ones."

Herman stood back. And with that, both Romey and Sam and the horses were enveloped by another mysterious cloud and felt themselves being transported somewhere once again.

When the cloud cleared, they and their horses were standing on the edge of a wooden drawbridge that led across a moat to the entrance of a castle wall.

"Whoosits!" Sam exclaimed. "I'll never get used to these quick changes. Now where are we?"

Romey immediately recognized where she was. Who could forget those heavy, twenty-foot high wooden double doors on the other side of the bridge, the large oval frame set in the wall surrounding a huge letter **R**. She remembered that the rounded towers extending upward on either side of the doors were so tall Romey almost fell over backwards, just like now, looking up at the red, cone-shaped tops where flags, each with a red **R,** still flapped in the wind. The castle walls, lower than the towers by half, still sparkled reds, yellows, greens, and blues from jewels embedded in them.

"We're back where I started," Romey answered. "Rairarubia Castle, right in the middle of the land of Rairarubia."

"Yes, now I remember. A terrible place."

"Now I think I understand the training we've been given. I think maybe I've known my purpose all along. And yours." Romey slowly nodded as she spoke.

"And what would that be?"

"To defeat the Mammoth."

Before Sam could ask what she meant, a bent figure in dirty, tattered clothes, walking with the use of a cane, approached them. His face was old and wizened.

"Romey, you must come with me." The voice sounded familiar to Romey.

"Where and why?" Romey asked cautiously.

"The Mammoth knows you two are near. He has doubled his guards. I will help you get in the castle without his knowing."

Romey thought the voice might be the one back in the cave where she accepted the testing.

"Knows we're here?" Sam questioned. "How could anybody know we're here, let alone who we are?" Sam didn't trust the old man. "And who is this Mammoth?"

"We have no time to waste. You both must come

with me now. You must trust me."

"Well, I don't," Sam protested flatly.

Romey looked into the old man's eyes and saw something that made her trust him. She knew now his was the voice from the cave.

"Let's go, then," she answered.

"Romey, are you going to trust this …"

Without another word, Romey, leading Black Arrow, began following the old man along the mote.

Sam stood there a minute, then muttered half to himself as he followed after them, "Okay, see if I care. But don't say I didn't warn you."

"And that's about as far as I've gotten with my ideas," Molly's father told them.

"And that's about enough for tonight anyway," her mother replied.

"So Romey's purpose is to fight the Mammoth?" Molly asked her father.

"Is that what you want it to be?"

Molly thought a moment. "I don't know exactly. It just seems like it ought to be more than that. I mean, did we create her just to have a fight with some big mean guy? Shouldn't all that training be for something more?"

"What do you want it to be for?" her mother asked. She was still worried that Molly was taking the Romey stories too seriously.

"Tell you what," her father offered, "you think of a purpose. You come up with the story tomorrow night, okay? That's your assignment from your old dad."

"I don't know if I can," Molly said, ignoring her mother's comments.

"Why not? Nobody knows Romey better than you."

Molly was to wonder about that comment long into the night.

CHAPTER 15

The next day, Molly had a terrible time concentrating on school work. Mr. Bly, her English teacher, had to call her name several times before she realized she was being called. That was so embarrassing.

Then Netty got all mad because she wouldn't eat lunch with her. Molly knew it sounded lame when she told Netty she wanted to be alone so she could come up with a good purpose for Romey.

"A purpose for Romey?" Netty said in a snit. "That should be obvious! Her purpose is to drive you bonkers. You are like really, really weird, Molly."

Molly was sorry she ticked off Netty. But Molly wanted to be sure she could come up with a good purpose to tell her dad. Giving a purpose to the story might be the key to all that's been happening. So all day, she kept thinking about a good purpose for Romey. It had to be more than a fight with the Mammoth. Even Romey must think so after all that training.

But the worst part of the day was during history studies. Molly was supposed to be listening to a report on the Boston Tea Party. Instead, she was mindlessly flipping through pages in her history book. Then one page caught her attention. It was a picture of a medieval castle.

The picture captivated Molly. It looked exactly like Rairarubia Castle. There stood the towers, the entrance, the bridge across the moat. The more she stared the more the castle seemed to grow larger, and larger, and larger. Until . . . .

Oddly, she heard the growing sounds of people. Not happy people, but people yelling and cursing. Then the smell began, the haze . . . .and there, just ahead walking along the bank of the moat . . . the three figures . . . the black and white horses . . . yes . . . there . . . then they disappeared into some tall brush along the bank . . . .

As all three crouched hidden in the bushes, the old man pointed across the moat to a iron grate covering an opening in the castle wall.

"Romey, you and Sam must make your way across the moat to that grate. Remove the grate and you'll find a small passageway you can crawl through that leads to the dungeon. You will find prisoners of Mammoth locked up. Overpower their guards and release the prisoners. You two must lead them against Mammoth. Believe me, they have every reason to want to help you."

"Just that simple, huh? Whoosits! You make it sound so easy." Sam didn't hide his sarcasm and doubt.

"But why us? Why are we the ones to do this?" Romey asked.

"All in good time, Romey."

"Somehow I just knew you were going to say that." Romey sighed. "Okay, but how do we get across the moat without being seen. I notice several guards walking along the wall up there." She pointed to the armed men walking back and forth.

The old man took out a small knife and cut several long, stiff reeds from the bush hiding them.

"Here, blow through these." He handed them each a long reed. When blown through, they cleaned out into hollow tubes.

"The reeds will allow you to breathe underwater. Keep under the surface, breathing through the reeds. The guards will never see you."

Sam looked at the reed he was holding. "You expect us to breathe through these skinny little straws? Why, whoosits, I'd rather take on an army!" He looked across the mote and doubted he could make it across. He hated the water and had never learned how to swim. The thought of going under water made Sam flush.

"Sam, this is the wrong time to get cold feet," Romey scolded.

"It's not cold feet I'm worried about; it's breathing."

"Is your companion up to the job?" the old man asked Romey. He looked toward Sam, worried. "Has there been a mistake in our choice?"

"Don't worry. He'll do it. He just likes to complain a lot."

Hearing the old man doubt his courage irked Sam. He felt as competent as Romey. And he didn't like being called a complainer, either.

"Ah, don't worry about me, old man. I'll do what I'm supposed to." But to himself, Sam wondered what other choice he really had.

"Then you must hurry. Time is running out. You must get to the prisoners and release them within the hour," the old man urged.

"Why the hurry?" Romey asked.

"The Mammoth plans to behead them in the square in front of the town's people." The old man looked even more solemn as he spoke the words.

"But why?" Sam asked before Romey could.

"Some because they spoke out against the Mammoth's cruelty and injustice. Some because they wouldn't bow to his authority. Others simply because the Mammoth may not have liked their looks. He is an evil man, not worthy of ruling Rairarubia. Nor is he the rightful ruler. Now hurry, you must go. I'll take care of your horses."

"Right. Well, let's go, Sam. Remember to breathe through your mouth, like this." Romey demonstrated, then watched Sam practice breathing through the reed.

"You got it. That's all there is to it."

Romey slid quietly into the water, followed by Sam. The fact that Romey seemed so certain the reeds would work eased Sam's concern some, but not entirely.

"Good luck," they heard the old man say as they felt themselves sinking underwater.

The moat water was dirty which made it difficult to see under the surface. Sam could barely make out Romey as she moved easily through the water. Even though the reeds worked, Sam could feel his heart thumping louder than usual. For him, the crossing seemed to never end. But within minutes, Romey and Sam reached the castle. Sam took in such a great breath of relief that Romey was afraid the guards might have heard. They waited a moment to make sure, then quietly started to work.

They had come up a little below the iron-bar grate, so had to hug themselves against the castle wall to get to it. Stuck tight, it took both of them to quietly pry the grate loose. Once loose, they let the grate sink into the moat.

Romey, heavy from wet clothes, hauled herself into the dark opening with Sam struggling after. Crawling carefully on hands and knees through the dank, narrow passage for several yards, they finally saw light ahead. Once at the end, they were confronted with another iron grill.

Romey peered through the bars into a room with a heavy wooded table and two crudely built chairs. Two torches burned on the opposite wall providing light in the windowless room. At first, Romey thought no one was there, but just as she was ready to try pushing on the grate, there came a cough.

Someone *was* in the room. Romey pulled back from the grate, bumping Sam's curious head who was leaning forward trying to see what he could. They both let out a slight noise and realized the danger if someone heard. They leaned tightly up against the passageway wall and almost breathlessly waited to see if they had been heard.

Two men came in view, but apparently they didn't

see Romey and Sam. The men sat down at the table and poured themselves a drink. But before they had a chance to drink, a voice from another room called out to them. The two men answered angrily, got up and disappeared from view again.

Romey and Sam heard a door slam and hoped that it meant the men had left the room. They waited a few moments and saw or heard no one.

"Let's go," Romey told Sam. Together they pushed, pulled, and finally kicked the grate loose and dropped to the floor of the room. They drew their swords, ready in case the guards heard them enter and returned.

There were two doors. Which one did the guards leave through? Which one should they try first?

Sam playfully pointed his sword at one then the other whispering, "Eeany, meany, miney, moe."

Romey shook her head at Sam and decided on the one on the right. She slowly opened the door and peeked through the crack. She saw men in cells and opened the door a little wider. It was the right one.

She and Sam pulled open the door and rushed inside ready to meet any more guards. Only one was in the room. He was so startled at their appearance he just stood there, unbelieving.

Romey and Sam had their swords pointed at his throat before he could recover his senses.

"The keys," Romey ordered.

The guard just shook his head.

Sam pushed his sword tighter against the man's throat. But before the captured guard could answer, a voice from one of the cells said, "On the wall. The keys are on the wall behind you."

Sam kept his sword at the guard's throat while Romey got the keys and began opening the cell doors. The men's spirits immediately were raised by their release, and their voices started to show it.

"Shhh. Keep your voices down. We still have to get

weapons for all of you," Romey warned.

"We knew you'd come," one of the men said. "Thank you." Others repeated the words as they gathered together outside the now empty cells.

"Then you knew more than I did," Romey replied. "I'd like to know *how* you knew, but not now. We don't have much time. Where do they keep the weapons?"

"In the armory. We'll have to go through the guards' quarters and that won't be easy," another man said.

"Show us the way," Romey told the men.

"Molly?"

Who was calling her name? She looked up from her history book, surprised she was still sitting in class.

"Did you hear the question, Molly? I asked if you could show us on the map?"

Molly felt the blood rush to her head as she turned red. She had no idea what Miss Turner was talking about.

"I—no." Molly's voice cracked.

"Well, now, I know you've been sick. Do you still feel ill? Something wrong?"

"No. I feel okay. I'm sorry. My mind was somewhere else."

"Ah, well, Molly, I think you'd better put your mind to getting caught up on what you've missed."

With that, Miss Turner called on someone else, and Molly slipped further down in her seat. She thought the heat in her cheeks would warm up the room by at least a hundred degrees.

She closed her history book and tried to forget Romey and concentrate on what Miss Turner was teaching.

It took forever for the school day to end. When it did, Netty caught up with Molly as they headed home.

"You were like totally out of it today—again. Look, if you need any help with homework to get caught up, I'll help you. Not that I'm such a whiz or anything."

"Thanks, Netty. Naw, I'll get caught up. I just got distracted by the picture of the castle in our history book. It's weird, I know, but it looks just like the castle we made up for Rairarubia."

"Castle? There's no picture of a castle in our history book. We're studying American history, remember?"

Oh, yeah? Well, look again, 'cause that's what got me in trouble today," Molly assured her.

CHAPTER 16

That evening, Molly confessed to her parents what had happened in school. Her embarrassment, however, was overshadowed by her excitement that a picture of Rairarubia castle was in her history book. She even got her history book to show them the picture of the castle, but for some reason she couldn't find it. She knew it must be in there, so she turned every page looking for it. But it just wasn't there anymore.

"It's not likely there would be a picture of a medieval castle in your American history book, Molly," her mother offered.

"That's what Netty said. But it *was* there, I swear. It looked just like Rairarubia Castle." Molly continued turning the pages, searching page by page. Without realizing it, she began telling them what happened as she stared into the picture.

"Romey and Sam met the voice in the cave, they swam the mote, crawled into the castle through the grate, released the prisoners." She rambled on as she flipped the pages. She saw her parents watch her, looking at each other, worried.

"Well, I hate to be the bad guy here, but I think these Romey stories have to stop."

"Oh, mom, no!" Molly looked at her father, wanting support.

But he showed a troubled expression and nodded his head in agreement. "It's one thing to have a vivid imagination, but when it starts interfering with your school work—well," his concerned voice trailed off.

Molly's stomach felt swooshy, her head a bit dizzy. Why couldn't she find the picture in her book? It was there in school. She couldn't have imagined that. Why was all this happening to her? Why *was* Romey on her mind so much? Everything was Romey, Romey Romey. Was she going to Romey, or was Romey coming to her? And what about the hidden arrowhead? Should she show it to her parents? The tears felt warm as they ran down her cheeks.

"Molly, honey, we only want to do what's best for you," her father added, noticing the tears.

To Molly, his comment sounded like an agreement with her mother: no more Romey. Then the tears really came.

"I never counted on any thing like this when we started the stories. It all seemed so harmless and fun." Her father sounded a bit confused himself.

"We just don't understand what's happening, dear." Her mother went over to Molly, putting her arm around her.

"Well, it's not Romey's fault," Molly sobbed.

"See, that's what we mean. You talk as if Romey were real. You seem obsessed with her." She held Molly's face in her hands. "She's always on your mind lately. The stories even bother your sleep. Now you're letting it trouble your school work. Don't you see why we're concerned?"

Molly nodded her head and leaned against her mother. She didn't know what to say. Lately, Romey *did* seem real, not someone she and her father had made up. She understood her parents' worry, but there was a pull toward Romey that even Molly didn't understand. If she couldn't explain it to herself, how could she explain it to her parents? But Molly knew, despite what her parents were saying, she couldn't stop thinking about Romey.

"What do you think we should do, Molly?" her father asked.

Molly wasn't sure where the words came from. "Finish the story. Finish it for good. It's almost over." Had she really said that? Yes, she wasn't sure how much more of the mystery she could handle.

Molly's parents looked at each other.

"What do you mean the story is almost over?" her father asked, a little mystified.

"If we finish the story, maybe everything will be over. I mean, then maybe I wouldn't think about Romey any more—or as much anyway." Molly hoped her parents would agree. Something she felt inside demanded the story be finished, with or without her parents. She was getting too confused.

After a moment, her father said, "Molly may be right. I think we should finish the story." Then he added, "To-night."

"I'm all for that," Molly's mother said.

Molly's moist eyes sparkled with her smile.

"But this is it, okay? This ends it." Her father smiled back and settled back into his chair. He hoped it would be so.

"So, you said," her father paused and Molly saw he was troubled by this, "that today Romey and Sam had just released the prisoners and were about to go to the armory to get weapons?" Her father helped put the pieces of her story together.

Molly nodded, leaning back against her mother as her father went on.

"Well, let's see now."

"This way, Romey," one of the men said, motioning her toward the door.

Romey stopped. "How do you know my name? Who are you?"

"I am Chance. But everyone knows who you are!" the man answered. All the men, now gathered around Romey and Sam, nodded and murmured agreement.

"But how?" Romey was puzzled.

"All that can be explained later. We must hurry or the guards will be suspicious," Chance urged.

Romey remembered what the old man outside the castle had said about the need to be quick. She looked at Sam, who just shrugged his shoulders.

"Okay, lead on, but there had better be some good answers later."

Chance put his finger to his lips and carefully opened the door. The corridor was empty. He motioned for Romey and Sam to follow. Close behind came all the released prisoners.

Another door stood closed at the end of the corridor. They could hear loud voices on the other side.

"The armory is in here," Chance whispered, then listened against the door. "Sounds like four or five men."

"Stand aside," Romey told him. "Sam and I will rush in and take the guards by surprise. All of you come charging in, but not too loudly. There may be more men around than we can handle. So get yourselves armed as fast as you can."

Chance moved aside while Romey and Sam took their positions at the door.

"Ready?" she asked.

Sam and the men nodded.

Romey and Sam rushed upon the door. Five men, sitting around a table, sat stunned and had no time to draw their weapons. Romey and Sam had their swords at the chests of two men. The men swarmed into the room and quickly began picking the weapons they wanted from the cache stored in the room.

Not a word was spoken, but within seconds, the one-time prisoners now held their guards captive.

"Chance, have a couple of the men lock these guards in the cells," Romey ordered.

"With pleasure." Chance motioned for two men to take the guards away.

"Now," Romey asked, "where's this Mammoth character?"

"I'm not sure, " Chance answered, "but I know we are supposed to be executed in the courtyard very soon now. More guards will be coming down to bring us up. Mammoth will certainly be there for the event."

"How do we get to the courtyard?" Romey asked.

"Two ways. One up the stairwell there, the other through that door and up the other side of the castle."

"Right. Then we'll split up. We still have surprise on our side. Sam, you take half the men and take the stairwell. I'll take Chance and the rest of the men the other way. Be careful. We don't know how many guards Mammoth has stationed between here and the courtyard. Make your way up to the castle walls and get rid of any guards up there—quietly. Then station your men around the walls so they cover the entire courtyard."

Sam nodded in agreement. "What are you going to do?"

"Once your men take the walls, it should be easy for us to control the courtyard. Let's hope the Mammoth is there. We'll give him a ceremony, all right, but not the one he's expecting."

Sam grinned. "Whoosits! I like it. Let's do it."

With that, Sam and his men disappeared up the stairwell.

"Okay, Chance, lead the way to the courtyard." Romey looked behind her and saw all the men armed and eager.

Romey was surprised how few guards they encountered on the way up. None of them gave her men any problems. They did not even seem eager to fight, just amazed, even willing to give up their weapons.

Once near one of the entries to the courtyard area, the men held back so they couldn't be seen. What they could see, though, was a raised wooden platform with a huge ax embedded in a chopping block. The men knew that the ax and chopping block were intended for the removal of their heads. Several of the men stroked their necks, happy their heads were still attached and more than ready to defend them.

Romey looked around the courtyard walls. Guards were still walking along the battlements. Had something happened to Sam? Why wasn't he up there? Fear that something had happened to Sam sent a wave of fear through her.

"Excuse me for interrupting," Molly's mother broke in, "But I think we'd better stop for dinner. Then we can finish this afterward. We are going to finish the story tonight, aren't we?" She raised her eyebrows at her husband. "Wasn't that the deal?"

"A promise is a promise. Okay, let's eat."

CHAPTER 17

After a quiet dinner, Molly and her parents shared doing the dishes and cleaning up the kitchen. Molly didn't feel much like talking and went about finishing her homework and catching up on what she had missed while sick. Even though Romey's thoughts occasionally crept into her studying, Molly found it a little easier to concentrate on her homework knowing there would be an end to the story tonight. At least, she hoped it would be the end.

When finished with her studies, she looked through her history book one more time, but still couldn't find the picture of the castle. Netty was right.

Then maybe there was never an arrowhead, either. Molly looked in the drawer where she had hidden it, hoping it wouldn't be there.

But there it was.

She covered it up again and slammed the drawer shut.

As Molly got ready for bed, she tried to remember where she could have gotten the arrowhead. But it was no use. The more she tried to remember, the more she began to believe it did come from Romey somehow. And she didn't want to think that. She wanted everything to be explained logically. Yes, her dad must finish the story. "It's got to be over," she told herself. "You can't keep imagining things."

Later, when she and her parents settled down on Molly's bed for the end of the story, she felt a anxious, like sitting a dentist's chair waiting to feel some pain that may or may not come.

"Now, let's see." Her father took a deep breath and began again.

The thought that something might have happened to Sam sent a wave of anxiety through Romey. Then she noticed one of the guards on the wall gave her a slight wave.

It was Sam. His men had disguised themselves in the guards' uniforms. They had made it after all.

Now, she thought with a bit of nervousness, bring on the Mammoth.

She didn't have to wait long. A blast of trumpets signaled Mammoth's arrival. From an entrance opposite Romey, out rode the Mammoth on his horse, his red cloak covering most of his dazzling white clothing. On his head, he wore a gold crown with a red triangular jewel set in the center. Behind him rode six warriors, dressed like some of the figures she had fought in training.

The Mammoth immediately sensed something was wrong.

"Where are the executioners? Where are the prisoners? Did I not order they be brought here at this time?" he bellowed in a voice that shook the ground.

Romey stepped out from where she was hiding, her voice barely loud enough to be heard. "There will be no execution."

"Who dares defy me?" The Mammoth rode closer to Romey. "Certainly not you, little one." The Mammoth threw his head back and laughed harshly.

"My purpose is to rid Rairarubia of you," Romey announced, taking a step forward.

"I think it is I who will rid Rairarubia of you." The Mammoth quit laughing and frowned. He stopped his horse when he was within a few feet of Romey and stared.

"Ah, yes, I've heard of you. You are Romey. And

the story goes that you will defeat me in battle."

Romey started to say, "So you've heard of me, too," but checked herself. Words weren't needed right now. Remember your training, she told herself. Your training brought you here.

The Mammoth broke a short silence between them. "I expected something different. I was led to believe I should fear you. I was wrong. You present no great challenge. You're but a mere girl."

He waved to his men behind him. "Take her away."

The six men quickly surrounded Romey on their horses.

At that moment, Sam yelled from the wall, "Fire!"

Instantly, the six men fell from their horses, their bodies full of arrows.

The Mammoth, taken by surprise, drew his sword and looked about. "Where are my guards? Who are those men on the walls?" he demanded, his horse stamping about excitedly.

"Where they belong," Chance replied, stepping from the shadows.

"So this is what they meant by my defeat. Well, I won't go that easily, Romey. If you are all they say you are, you will fight me in battle— alone. Not with all this help. We fight to the end, just you and me. If I win, I regain control of Rairarubia. If you win, well, that's not likely, but if you do, then the kingdom belongs to you."

"Don't do it, Romey," Chance said. "We've won. You don't need to do more."

"No," Romey replied. "It won't be over until I personally defeat the Mammoth. I know that is my purpose, the reason for my training, for the powers given me."

"Powers? And what powers would those be, little upstart?" The Mammoth jeered. "I have some powers of my own. I'll show you real power."

With that, the Mammoth jumped from his horse, and before everyone's astonished eyes, he split into six separate Mammoths! They surrounded Romey, each one laughing and jeering at her.

But they spent too much time sneering and scoffing at Romey. It gave her time to pull out the pouch with the magic dust in it. She quickly sprinkled some all around her, muttering to herself, "Nothing can harm me, right, Herman? Oh, boy, you'd better be right about this stuff."

"That's your power? That's supposed to stop me?" All six of him said. "Ha!" And with that they all charged at Romey, swords raised. But when they brought their swords down in unison, they clanged against an invisible barrier.

The surprised resistance caused all six Mammoths to vibrate so hard they lost form, each slipping back into one body. Unbelieving, the frowning Mammoth raised his sword again, then swung it at Romey's head with all his might.

Clang — ang — ang!

The sword broke when it hit the barrier protecting Romey. The shock of the blow jarred the Mammoth's crown off his head.

"It worked," Romey cried out as she stepped from the ring of magic. "Now who's laughing?" she asked the Mammoth as she pointed her sword at him.

With his sword in pieces, the Mammoth jumped on his horse and headed for the gateway to the bridge over the moat. To every one's surprise, Romey sat down and began taking off her boots.

All the men began shouting after the Mammoth as he sped through the gate. They couldn't believe their eyes. There sat Romey changing her shoes while the Mammoth got away!

"Romey," Sam yelled from his position on the wall, "he's getting away."

"Not today, he isn't," Romey muttered as she slipped on the magic leather moccasins tucked inside her shirt. She barely stood up before she seemed to disappear before the onlookers' eyes.

Mammoth, thinking he was free and clear as he crossed the bridge, suddenly saw Romey running along side his horse. She reached for the horse's reins and yanked hard. The confused horse slowed and then suddenly stopped, throwing Mammoth over the horse's head.

But Mammoth surprised Romey again. As he was thrown from his horse, he spread his red cape and flew through the air for several yards, landing on the other side of the moat.

Romey wasted no time and leaped high over the moat and landed next to Mammoth. With sword still in hand, she swung at the red cape.

The cape fell to the ground, but nothing was under it. Mammoth had disappeared. Romey could not believe it. She looked all around, confused. There was no place to hide, making it all the more mysterious.

By this time, Sam and many of the men had caught up with Romey.

"He disappeared!" Romey told them in disbelief. "He just plain disappeared!" She angrily jabbed her sword into the ground.

"But where?" Sam puzzled. "This is all open field. How could he just disappear?"

"He has great magical powers," Chance said sadly. "It is not good that he is free. I have seen his evil. I have witnessed what he can do. But people say his powers are connected to this cape. Strange he would leave it behind."

As Chance was talking, he bent down and picked up the cape. Romey noticed a slight movement on the ground where the cape had been. There, no larger than two inches high, was Mammoth.

Romey reached down and picked him up as he tried to run. "Well, he doesn't look very harmful right now." She held him up for all the men to see. The sight of the great Mammoth caught in Romey's hand started the men laughing.

"What are we going to do with him?" Sam asked.

"I know exactly what to do. Here, hold him. Bring me a bow and arrow."

While Sam held Mammoth tight, Romey put on her magic leather gloves. Then she pulled a loose thread from her shirt.

"Hold him up against the arrow," Romey directed Sam. Then she began tying Mammoth to the arrow shaft.

"What are you doing? Give me back my cape! Let me go!" Mammoth could barely be heard, even though he was yelling as he squirmed.

"Yes, what exactly *are* you doing?" Sam looked puzzled.

Romey just smiled. When she felt Mammoth was firmly tied to the arrow, she placed it in her bow string and pulled back as far as she could.

"What are you doing? Untie me! Fight like a man!" Mammoth squealed.

"Whoosits! You wouldn't—you are!" Sam laughed. Everyone was howling with delight.

"Magic gloves, send this arrow out of the land of Rairarubia where it will never find its way back."

With that, Romey let the arrow fly. With a twang and a whoosh, the arrow, and Mammoth with it, sped into the sky.

Cheers from all the released men thundered as the arrow disappeared from view. Their cries of happiness brought out people who before had been too afraid.

Making his way through the crowd came the old man who had shown Romey and Sam the passageway into the castle. He led both Black Arrow and White Arrow by the reins. After he handed the horses over to their owners, the old man held up the crown that Mammoth had worn for all to see. The crowd grew silent. Then the old man spoke.

"This is the crown of evil. It has brought misery and pain to our land."

Then he pried the red triangle ruby from the crown and held the sparkling jewel up for all to see. Quiet murmurs of agreement went through the crowd.

"This is the jewel of freedom! It has been trapped in the crown until someone could liberate it!" he announced. Then he walked over to Romey and asked her to show her medallion. She pulled it from her shirt and watched as the old man placed the ruby in the last setting. The medallion was now complete. The four rubies seemed to shine more brilliantly than ever. The gold crown, without the jewel, crumbled into nine small, colorful pebbles.

"Look at that!" Sam said as he bent down and picked them up. "How could that be?"

The old man didn't answer, but dropped on one knee and loudly announced, "Queen Romey, ruler of Rairarubia!"

Soon Romey was surrounded by the happy people of Rairarubia. Chance lead the group into a chant as they kneeled before her.

"Three cheers for Queen Romey!"

"Hip, hip, hooray! Hip, hip, hooray! Hip, hip, hooray!"

Sam whispered to Romey, "Whoosits! You never told me you were a queen."

"I never knew it before myself." Romey was stunned.

"Well, *I'm* not bowing to you," Sam told her defiantly.

"No one is," she told him. Romey raised her arms and called for the crowd to be quiet.

"Please," she shouted, "never bow down before me again. You are free people. For a long time now I have not known what my training was for, my true purpose, but now I do. Getting rid of Mammoth was only part of it. Together we will make the land of Rairarubia a rich and happy place for all. That's my ..." she looked at Sam " ... *our* ... real purpose."

The people roared with approval.

"Sam, I'm going to need all the help I can get," she told him as she mounted Black Arrow. "I've got a feeling our real purpose and tests are just beginning."

"I guess I understand my purpose now, too. You and me, we're a team, like I said. Well, there's a lot of work to do, shall we get at it?"

Sam mounted White Arrow, and the pair rode across the bridge and into the castle as the happy crowd of people followed, still cheering.

Unseen to Romey and Sam were Bovert, Herman, and a hooded figure standing on the sidelines.

"She will make a great queen," said Bovert, watching the procession into the castle. "She is indeed the chosen one."

"Yes," Herman replied, "and Sam will make a fine king."

The hooded figure seemed to communicate a message to both Bovert and Herman without speaking a word. They nodded in understanding, turned and followed the crowd into the castle.

"So, how's that for a happy ending?" Molly's father asked.

"Good. I like it," Molly answered.

"Well, I'm just relieved it's over," her mother said. "I know I'm repeating myself, but I think you two created more than you bargained for."

Molly's father laughed, "That's for sure. All because our daughter here was bored." He gave Molly a tuck under her chin.

"Well, I can't say I've been bored much since Romey arrived." Molly sighed.

"No," her mother said, "in fact, it's almost like we've had another member of the family with us. Well, now that we've put Romey to bed, so to speak, let's put you to bed."

Her parents kissed Molly goodnight, turned out the light, and left her alone.

Molly lay in bed, too awake to sleep. Was it really over? Was that the end of Romey and Sam and the land of Rairarubia? There were still some unanswered questions as far as she was concerned. While she wanted to tell her parents about the arrowhead, she just didn't know how.

Molly waited for her eyes to adjust to the dark. Once she could make out things in her room, she went to her dresser to get the hidden arrowhead.

But what was this? Something else was there, too. Where had it come from?

She picked up a small leather pouch, like a marble bag, and moved to a better light by the window. Molly spread the thongs that held the bag closed and dumped the contents into her hand.

Out fell nine small, colorful pebbles.

THE END ?

Will Molly discover where the leather pouch
containing nine pebbles came from?

Look for *The Return to Rairarubia* and find out.